WEEKEND AT THE VILLA

By the same author under the name Dorothy Palmer Hines
NO WIND OF HEALING

WEEKEND AT THE VILLA

DOROTHY QUINTANO

PUBLISHED FOR THE CRIME CLUB BY
DOUBLEDAY & COMPANY, INC.
GARDEN CITY, NEW YORK
1974

All the characters in this book are fictitious, and any resemblance to actual persons, living or dead, is purely coincidental.

Quintano, Dorothy.
  Weekend at the villa.

  I. Title.
PZ3.Q4577We   [PS3533.U697]   813'.5'4
ISBN: 0-385-06752-6
Library of Congress Catalog Card Number 73–11718

First Edition

Copyright © 1974 by Dorothy Quintano
All Rights Reserved
Printed in the United States of America

This book is for our real-life Francesca from her mother—
with love.

WEEKEND
AT THE VILLA

CHAPTER ONE

The moment I saw the great, bulging fieldstone gatehouse that guards the entrance to the Park rising ahead in the misting rain, I had that same quivering tremor of anxiety that even the mention of the name Villa Belsola always managed to evoke.

I moved closer to my brother, Nikki, clutching my navy canvas tote bag as though it were some magic talisman and huddled deeper in the recesses of our stepfather's chauffeur-driven car.

I kept trying to remind myself of Nikki's reassurance: "Francesca," he'd kept insisting, "just think of this as an ordinary weekend visit in the country." So while I struggled to sustain a widely paced dialogue between us, about anything and everything, we hadn't even noticed the dreary village of Sloatsburg slide past. As for the village of Tuxedo itself—notable as a speed trap for unwary tourists headed for the Catskills via Route 17—one would have to look sharp or miss it completely.

The village, which approximated about three city blocks, consisted chiefly of a beauty shop, liquor store and the ancient fieldstone post office. Behind this cluster, on the right side of the road, ran the commuters' Erie railroad and on the left side the stone ramp leading to the only market in the village, the low red brick library building with its white trim and multi-faceted windows and, of course, the pseudo-Tudor building that housed a hardware and drugstore on the first level and on the second, behind cramped dormer windows, a dentist's office. It was only then, as the car slowed at the approach to the Park, that we both fell silent.

It was ten years since Nikki and I had first come to Villa Belsola. Nikki was twelve and I was ten yet the memory of our father's death, which had sent us—Mummy, Nikki and me—to seek refuge in our Grandfather Bascome's home, was still sharply . . . painfully . . . clear. More painful still was the bitter memory of the tragedy that followed. Villa Belsola had proved not a haven but a grim nightmare.

The car swung toward the Park gatehouse, a guard peered through a misting pane, rubbed a clear spot on the glass cubicle then waved on the long, gray Bentley through the iron gates and toward the villa.

I looked toward Nikki for reassurance, but he kept his eyes fixed straight ahead. I had to satisfy myself with my own reflection in the car window which gave back the image of a girl much younger than my years. However, I was beginning to be used to being mistaken for a teenager. This is mostly, I think, because I wear junior petite clothes. Then, too, my new hair style, which I'd hoped would lend some air of sophistication, seemed only to accentuate the youthful image.

I had just had my hair shaped and shortened into something called "the swinger." Nikki assured me I did, indeed, look a swinger. Something I felt it unnecessary to remind him I did not in the least feel. In any case, I was glad I'd settled on the yellow cotton miniskirted suit and matching sandals—as they seemed to lend the only streak of color in this entire drab landscape.

The late summer rain which had been falling ceaselessly the whole day seemed to gather momentum now as we took the curve around the narrow tortuous road that skirted the lake.

The lake . . . I glanced once quickly, at Nikki, feeling a sick lurching in the pit of my stomach, wondering whether he would have the courage to look toward the lake or would he, for all of his visit here, keep his eyes averted from that dismal body of water that had been dragged and dredged to recover our beautiful mother's fragile body.

How innocent that calm expanse of water appeared now, punctured by great pelting drops of rain. Nestling in the lush greenery, the scene had almost the dreamlike quality of a Corot. Very different from that frenzied scene of police dockside and the shouting and hauling and dredging that had catapulted Nikki into a miasma of silence and fear. For a while, it was thought Nikki might never regain his speech. The experience almost too traumatic for him to be able to sustain. But he was well now. I moved closer to him. He was well. I had to keep reminding myself of this and forget all the rest.

I looked away from the lake and pretended an interest and curiosity I did not feel about the moving landscape. Overhead trees dripped, windshield wipers swept a monotonous rhythm, while all around us the Ramapo Mountains were shrouded in glowering, night-dark clouds. A station wagon with small children in yellow slickers doused its headlights at us in greeting as it passed.

Occasionally, the tip of a brick chimney pierced the green, or a stone gate was visible from the road. Driveways wound up and up and up to houses hidden behind tall hedges and dripping foliage. Names long forgotten were recalled—Bakers, Hamiltons, De Meyers—Senior and Junior. Or Gull's Nest, Shadow Lake, Miramar. As we continued to tunnel our way through the dripping overhead leaves of arched trees I thought what a long way this was in time as well as distance from my little walk-up apartment on East Eighty-first.

I had been living in that apartment for two years when Nikki returned from India. The apartment was great. A remodeled building with a store front cut out of the once ground-floor apartment, now occupied by two rather Mod gals who created original and rather way-out clothes which they made themselves and sold along with odd bits of jewelry, fashion foolery, and psychedelic posters. Squeezed on the other side was an upholsterer whose windows were crowded with exquisite fabrics, naked and stripped-down frames of chairs and love seats and flaps of remnants and remnant books and a small penciled card stuck in the window indicating the proprietor was available between three and six each day. In my two-year residence, I had never seen him. Or a customer. I concluded he must traffic in girls, or drugs, or possibly both!

My apartment was on the top floor and there was a kind

of skylight in the outside corridor. And as I was the only tenant on the top floor I would often keep the door open to use this as an extension of my studio. The light was perfect and so long as I was able to circumvent the fire department my little studio was safe. I had a job on *Sortie,* the magazine for young career females and I continued to sketch at the Art Students League. I told myself so long as I continued to sketch I would grow as an artist. So three nights a week I'd walk over from my office on East Fifty-fifth Street, cut across the vacant lot by the School for Young Professionals and come out by the Russian Tea Room across from the League. The only break in my routine was an occasional dinner with Aunt Virginia and Uncle Willie Trent. This was only a polite formality, as neither Virginia nor Willie, I was sure, really wanted to have anything to do with the eccentric Fabriolli-Grazzis: Our family name, which Nikki and I had contracted to Grazzi in the hope people would be less apt to associate that name—and us—with all the unhappy family notoriety. Virginia, rather like our Grandfather Bascome, had never quite forgiven Mother for marrying our father. The ill-fated consequences were to her mind only what should have been expected. Indeed, I often felt she considered our parents had only got their just deserts. But maybe I was being harsh on them. Anyway, our relationship was only a kind of lip service harking back to that time when they'd taken me to live with them, temporarily, when our mother died. But my real life was centered in my art and my concern for Nikki.

I dated occasionally but was not serious about anyone.

Probably the only male that had serious intentions toward me was Peter. Peter Wright, a young man whom I'd met at the League. He was incredibly conservative by League standards and I often felt a bit sorry for him for the ribbing he took when, after classes, we'd all get together in the cafeteria and over coffee discuss art, politics, and sex. However, once I'd seen his work I stopped feeling sorry for him and so did everyone else. He was a very real talent. And though in many ways he remained an outsider because of his almost Ivy League manner and his speech —Boston Brahmin laced with Harvard—his talent earned everyone's respect. On our dates, he invariably deferred to me and I always tried to think up some out-of-the-way place for us to dine. I think it was sort of a game I played to see if I could shake him up. But he trailed after me faithfully from the Inca, down in the city's meat-packing section, to watching old men play boccie as we dined off mouth-watering veal at Il Vagabondo.

Mostly I think I kept seeing Peter because it *is* flattering to have an attractive, eligible young male in love with one. Then, too, I considered him a challenge. There had to be something more behind that face to produce such remarkable work. Once or twice he made an effort to get me up to Boston over a holiday. It was tacit this was to meet his family. I couldn't begin to consider anything like that. Finally, he stopped asking me. I never knew whether it was because he finally accepted my feelings for him for what they were or he was responding to pressure from his family who must surely have remembered all the unpleasant notoriety associated with the tragedies in our family. None of this was important, though, so long as Peter and I could maintain our friendship. He was fun and strikingly good-looking if you went in for that Brooks Brothers preppy image. Peter, in fact, was the only one of the League crowd whom I especially wanted to see Nikki's photos . . . and the show was tomorrow. This was one of the reasons I couldn't understand Nikki's insistence on this trip up here. The most important thing for me right now was his show. This place meant nothing to me, nothing but unhappiness. It was a whole other world, removed from us.

CHAPTER TWO

We had first come to the Villa Belsola after our father had been killed in a street mugging. Our mother, in quiet desperation, not knowing which way to turn, had fled with us to her father's ornate Italianate villa in Tuxedo Park. Here she felt her children at least would find comfort and peace. But there had been no peace for us anywhere. One tragedy followed another.

I remember the first day we came to the villa. It had been raining that day, too. It was early fall and the first leaves whipped from the trees had flattened themselves in red and yellow patches along the macadam highway and on the hood of our car while torrents of rain poured down the windows. Our mother said, "The heavens weep for us. . . ." and sat straight and slim, crowded in the back seat with us, looking unbelievably young and fragile in her new widow's weeds. The back seat was crowded with packing cases and odds and ends that could not fit into the trunk, so I knew we were not on a visit to our Grandfather Bascome's but were coming here to live. We were leaving that huge city apartment on the fifteenth floor where I could remember many days when I was not able to go outdoors, and Nella, our nursemaid, would hold me aloft, my face pressed against the window pane while I tried to see Mummy and Nikki, tiny little figures below, making their way across the Avenue toward Central Park. We had been happy there. And, then, all the way on our trip up here even Biscuit, our mother's dog, lying curled on the floor of the car on our mother's walk-in-the-rain coat, kept one eye alerted and one ear cocked for some signal. Sometimes she whimpered and growled a little in her throat and our mother would lean over and run her slim finger along Biscuit's nose, then outline one ear with a gentle caress to quiet her.

Neither Nikki nor I spoke. Nikki looked very pale in a white shirt under his gray blazer. He wore a black tie. I shall always remember that sad, ugly black tie.

The trees whirled by in a moving mass of wet, riotous colors when, suddenly, at a turn in the road, there was Sieppi. He stood along the driveway leading to the villa, in all the torrents of rain, wearing the same odd outfit which we would come to associate with him, and, touching his hat as the car approached, dipped his knee in a gesture that was almost like genuflecting while he held out an enormous bouquet of roses to our mother.

Mummy had Dudley stop the car and opened the door herself. A great gust of rain blew in on us as she leaned forward to accept the rain-drenched crimson roses. He spoke to her in a soft dialect. He was welcoming our mother home in all her sorrow. Our mother's eyes filled a little. Darling Sieppi . . . He was the single happy memory, after our mother died, that I had of the villa.

After Mummy's marriage to Phelps, everything changed. There were no more days spent together up in the guest room. Then it was the room in which she enjoyed painting because it looked out over the garden and the chapel and away beyond to the Ramapo hills. Our grandfather was constantly urging her to let him fix up the guest cottage for her. "The entire cottage," he told her, "could be made over just to your liking into your very own studio. You could work there without interruption. You could accomplish some real work there."

"Ah, Pa . . ." Our mother would lean her cheek caressingly against her father's, her long, silken blond hair falling forward over her face, "I'm not an artist. I'm a dilettante. I should be inhibited in a real studio. I like this just painting and messing around here in my own, odd way."

And she did. We used to race up to the room once school was out to see if this was a day she would be there painting, anticipating our joy to find her there. She'd order tea sent up for us, making a face with her lips drawn down tight behind Mrs. Dudley's back as the dour housekeeper served it. Everything Mrs. Dudley did for us seemed such a chore. The "dour Dudley" Mummy called her behind her back, winking at us. Sometimes when it was getting on to five and the light was no longer good for painting Mummy'd have her cocktail sent up with our tea. Later, the cocktail hour got pushed up to four o'clock. But that was later. Things were altogether different after Phelps came.

Grandpa brought Phelps home for dinner one night. He insisted our mother was being morbid, refusing to leave the villa even to visit old friends in the Park. Some of the old friends used to say that they bet old man Bascome wished he'd never bought that great ornate villa, that maybe in a more rugged environment—say Tudor, perhaps —Liz might not have lingered so long with her memories of her husband.

What Nikki and I hadn't known, of course, was that it had been harder for our mother to return the repentant daughter than to face the reality of her husband's having been mugged, beaten, and killed just two blocks from where we'd lived.

The tabloids had a field day. They showed pictures of our father looking tanned and elegant as captain of the polo team and then horrible pictures, which everyone tried to hide from Nikki and me, his body lying in the gutter covered by a blanket while cameramen flashed bulbs. A Sunday supplement ran a feature article about the families. It was then Nikki and I discovered it had been generally assumed Phelps Warton was going to marry our mother. But somewhere along the way, Phelps had introduced her to our father. After that, she had eyes for no one but Daddy.

There were pictures of our mother making her debut . . . "The lovely Liz Bascome, heiress to the Bascome Bread fortune, escorted by Phelps Warton. . . ." Everywhere she went, Phelps was right alongside her and people began to say what wonders she had done for Phelps who, up until then, had had a kind of reputation of being a playboy. Cholly Knickerbocker, who wrote a society column avidly read by those who followed the scene, carried an item that, "Any day now rumor has it Liz Bascome,

heiress to the family Bascome Bread fortune will step right up to the altar and into the Register on the arm of Phelps Warton, society's most eligible bachelor. . . ."
While a few pages over in the same paper a columnist devoted to the night life circuit of the city predicted that, "A bevy of beauties from the night club circuit will be chief mourners at the Bascome-Warton nuptials and the race track crowd are already thinking of initiating a Phelps Warton Day to commemorate their loss . . . not to mention the bookies, themselves . . ."

But our mother eloped instead with our father. Theirs had been a romantic and idyllic marriage. They seemed only to need each other but willingly made room in their lives for us children.

We had never even visited the villa. Our mother would make allusions occasionally to her childhood in the Park; sharing memories of her pony and cart, and Sieppi the gardener. They were more like bedtime stories that parents who have had happy childhood memories share with their children. Very possibly because of this, even in our sadness, there was a feeling of expectancy, a sense that some joy might lie ahead waiting for us at the villa.

When, finally, our mother married Phelps, gossip had it that our Grandfather Bascome, whose driving ambition had sent the family fortune soaring, had manipulated our mother into this marriage. It was what he had wanted from the first and quite possibly was his condition for "forgiveness." He had finally arrived socially. This marriage had done for him what his money could not. He arrived in time to die, but supposedly to someone like Hiram Bascome the sweet taste of success is all that matters.

He had the first of the two coronaries that were finally to prove fatal. It was then Phelps and Mother were married. He wanted to know his darling Elizabeth was settled and the children cared for. He left his entire property and most of his income to "my darling Elizabeth so she may make a new life in that environment she has always known and loved."

Everyone seemed to feel he had been fair with Aunt Virginia and Uncle Willie, leaving them stocks and some cash and securities, since they were childless and had more or less settled on a life in town. Whatever his reasoning, this is how our grandfather left things, so we went right on living at Villa Belsola just as we had after our father's death, only now there was Phelps.

I remember when Mummy told us about the marriage, acting kind of apologetic, explaining how it was. I remember Nikki's white face. It was whiter than the day of our father's funeral. He looked so thin, too. The way children do, somehow, when they have just gotten over a long illness and have suddenly shot up and everything seems too small for them. His thin, knobby wrists hung below his sleeves and his eyes were gleaming as though he had a fever. He didn't say anything. He just ran off. Mummy was very upset, but I tried to explain how it was with Nikki. I told her he was probably going to cry and he was ashamed for her to see. Hot tears of rage, I supposed. But I explained how pretty soon he would go off with his camera to comfort him and would be lost in his world of picture taking, looking for new sites, possibilities for his pictures and then he would calm down. The storm would be over. There wasn't anything Mummy or I could do to help him.

Nikki was always like that, difficult to help. Even on the day he most needed help. That day. The day it happened. It was really like every other day. The way it always seems to be when you look back on some tragedy. You can say the mail came as usual that day. I walked the dog as usual that day. It was like every other day. There was no school. I slept a little later than usual and then got into a shirt and Bermuda shorts and started out to join Nikki if I could find him. As I started down the long hall I noticed from a window along the corridor that there was a car parked in the driveway. I hadn't heard it arrive so I couldn't tell how long it might have been there. And I remember thinking it wasn't a car I recognized, that belonged to anyone I knew, and the license was different. A different color from the New York State license. By the time I reached the second landing the car had gone. I hadn't heard any voices but then these houses were built to muffle most sounds. Actually, it was only the dinner gong, which reverberated through the entire house, that we could hear. We couldn't even hear the telephone—Nikki and I—in our wing of the house.

As I started down the wide stone stairs, I picked up their voices. I stopped. I didn't want to eavesdrop. This wouldn't be the first quarrel I'd overheard. There had been many. Our mother's voice strained and angry. Or pitiful as a child's, waiting for Phelps's verbal barrage to fall. I was glad in a way, if there had to be a quarrel, that I was alone. That Nikki was out there somewhere in the wild acreage of the Park, tending to his camera and his pictures.

Once before there'd been a quarrel when Mummy had been drinking too much. From our perch on the top of the stairs, the sound of her feet said she was staggering a little and Phelps had rung for Mrs. Dudley. "Don't," he had told Mother, "try to navigate those stairs, Liz, you'll break your neck." And he must have reached for her because I heard her slurring "Leggo' a' me . . ." I felt Nikki tensing beside me and I had to put my arm out across him, where he sat huddled on the stairs, so he would not try to go down. From the servants' quarters we had watched Mrs. Dudley coming along, her mouth drawn down in that same tight curve of disapproval, patting the bun at the nape of her neck, smoothing down her apron before she knocked, then entered. Through the thin wedge of light from the opened door we saw Phelps, his face flushed and angry. "Ah, Mrs. Dudley, Mrs. Warton is not feeling well. She'll have a tray upstairs."

"Very good, sir. May I help you, madame."

"Oh . . . no you don'." We heard our mother distinctly, her voice shrill. "You don' wanna' help me. Never did. Oney Ginny . . . Your lil' Ginny, tha's the one you always have to help." She mocked Mrs. Dudley's Scots burr. *"Ah . . . there's the pet . . .* You never liked me. Not ever."

"Come on, Liz, don't be absurd. You'll hurt Mrs. Dudley's feelings."

"Ah, that'll be the day. Leggo!" The door opened again

and Nikki and I had flattened ourselves against the wall so as not to be seen as she pulled away from Phelps again. Phelps handed her over to Mrs. Dudley.

"Tsk . . . tsk . . ." Mummy said, "you don' like having to try and keep your little secrets do you, Dudley . . . Dudley has a secret . . . Dudley has a secret," our mother singsonged now. And the look on Mrs. Dudley's face sent a shiver through me. At that moment, I think, Mrs. Dudley could have killed our mother.

Nikki had turned his face against the wall and was crying. I pretended I didn't see. He cried for our mother. He could not bear to see her like this. Nikki hated it when our mother drank too much. Yes, I thought, remembering that scene, it was good Nikki was not around to hear this quarrel.

"You coward . . . you filthy coward. No, get away from me! Get back or I'll kill you, I mean it." Our mother must have picked up something—the fire tongs, some weapon—and was brandishing it at Phelps because when he next spoke his voice was quiet, almost cajoling.

"Liz, honey, don't be crazy. Let me explain. Put that thing down."

"Explain! How could you explain anything. How can you explain murder. You're a murderer. *Murderer. . . .*" She screamed at him. There was a crash. The sound ripped through me. I saw her race out the side door through the garden, her slender, sun-tanned legs flashing in the tennis shorts, her blond hair flying. She was headed toward the lake.

I put my head down between my legs to stop the shaking and the waves of nausea. She would be all right now. Like Nikki, she had gone off to find solace. Her comfort was the water and her dinghy. By the time she had crossed the lake and come back again in the glittering morning sunlight, she would have calmed down. She would come back to the house, change for lunch, have cocktails on the terrace, and the whole crazy pattern of her days would begin all over again.

It was after noon hour. I heard the rattle of lunch dishes in the pantry. Mrs. Dudley was arranging the flowers for the luncheon table on the terrace when I heard, "My God, mon, what's happened?" I looked out to see Dudley coming up the path from the lake carrying Nikki in his arms. I raced down and was at the edge of the terrace when he arrived.

"Nikki, Nikki!" I went to throw myself on him but Mrs. Dudley grabbed me and held me in a tight grip, her arm across my chest. Her face was ashen.

"Nikki, Nikki, what's the matter . . . *Nikki. . . .*" I screamed.

"He'll be O.K., miss. He's had a terrible"—Dudley paused—"a most terrible shock." He motioned to Mrs. Dudley, who sank abruptly into the nearest chair, almost dragging me into her lap.

"There's been a terrible accident, Frannie, girl. A terrible accident," Dudley said. "Here, let me get the boy upstairs."

It was only later when Phelps returned and the house was swarming with police and the rescue crew that I understood the accident was not to Nikki but to our mother.

Death by drowning was the coroner's final verdict. But not before weeks and weeks of probing and questioning as to why a young woman so capable a swimmer, so able with a boat should have drowned in a calm as glass lake in the early hours of a summer morning. There were nasty whispers and rumors of suicide. Suicide? Our mother? It was unthinkable. Yet, I knew, young as I was, that there would always be those rumors our mother had taken her own life. How Nikki was to react to this was something I dared not contemplate. For darling Nikki adored our mother, if it was possible, more than anyone else. And so it evolved that I was shipped off to stay with Aunt Virginia and Uncle Willie, while Nikki had to be sent to that special school to try and regain his speech.

CHAPTER THREE

It was only logical, I supposed, that the return to the villa, fraught with such mixed memories, would naturally evoke all the old emotions. As the car swung between the stone pillars that formed an archway guarded by a sculptured lion embracing a stone shield and we headed along the yew-lined drive, I felt if I closed my eyes I could see myself, like film unwinding backward, being bundled by Uncle Willie into the big black limousine. The slam of the car door, then the yew trees spinning backward, leaving everything behind us, while he returned me to New York and Aunt Virginia. Very probably it had been one of the hired funeral cars as Uncle Willie did not drive. That was another of the things he abominated along with F.D.R., left-wing radicals, and Daylight Saving Time which he perceived as some kind of Communist plot! Virginia had already gone back to the apartment ahead of us. I'd done all of my packing and most of Nikki's, although Mrs. Dudley had insisted on helping. I could see her, even now, patting and folding all the not-to-be-forgotten essentials into Nikki's suitcase that lay opened on his bed. The way she folded everything into neat little piles you'd think she was preparing a picnic basket. And I remember that sudden sense of finality as though I was only then beginning to understand what was happening to us. Nikki and I were going to be separated! I could feel hot tears and my throat closing, but I didn't want Nikki to know. He stood watching us pack, never offering to help not even when it came to his camera equipment. In fact, he turned his face away as I fitted the tripod, flash gun, and other gear into the kit, as though this was a part of him that hurt and the pain was insupportable. Although I understood he had to go off to this special school and I would be going to live with Aunt Virginia and Uncle Willie, and probably attend Miss Stiles's School where Mummy and Aunt Virginia had gone before me, nevertheless, I did not really quite realize what had happened to Nikki, and I would grab at him, digging my fingers into his arm as though I could squeeze some sound from him. "Nikki, Nikki, say something. Say something to me, Franca . . . please, Nikki." But he simply loosened my hand separating my fingers one by one from his arm and turned away, gently. It was as though there were no more rage and anger left inside him—only hurt. Soon after he had gone off to Brookhaven, and I'd settled in with Virginia and Willie, Aunt Virginia came into my room one night and sitting on the edge of my bed and speaking as though it were a part she had rehearsed, said, "Francesca, your uncle and I know it must be very difficult for you to understand about your brother. We wish we could help. It is difficult to know"—her face cracked into a kind of conspiratorial smile—"why one person can cope, has the stamina to face things and another has not. You had a very tragic experience with the loss of your father and now this dreadful thing—your mother's death." She leaned over and patted my hand. I dug myself deeper under the covers. "We can't, any of us, know *why* Nikki can't cope, has so fragile a—, aa—." Poor Aunt Virginia, I think she hoped I would help her out. But I couldn't. Even if I had wanted to I couldn't, because the sense of loss, the absence of Nikki, was like being engulfed in a wave of enormous sadness. I realized she was trying to be helpful and sympathetic and maybe she felt sorry for being so spiteful about our mother and father. But I just wished she'd go away. "Well, dear," she tucked the covers up under my chin and switched off my bedside light. "I just wanted you to know we understand and try not to worry about Nikki. He's in good hands and I'm sure he'll come round very quickly." *Come round . . . ?* What a curious choice of words. As though Nikki were just being arbitrary and when all these competent doctors got through with him they'd manage to show him the error of his ways. I kicked at the bedclothes, throwing them off, the single gesture I could muster to show my rebellion. Couldn't they understand Nikki was suffering, too, in a different way? I was as much a prisoner in this apartment as Nikki was at that school. We belonged together. These weren't our kind of people. Sometimes, nights, after dinner, when Uncle Willie sat glued to his *Wall Street Journal* and Aunt Virginia was working her endless, always-to-be-completed needlepoint, bellpulls and footstool covers, I'd stare around the room and wonder how we could possibly be related to these people. But, there, spread across the shiny Mason and Hamlin baby-grand piano was the evidence—a family picture gallery; childhood studio portraits of Mummy and Virginia, dressed alike in their flowered, smocked, Liberty print frocks, arms entwined, their slender, tanned legs dangling down in little barefoot sandals. In the folding, hand-tooled leather frames, brought back by the dozen from tours of Florence, were snapshots of Grandpa Bascome at the villa, with the dogs, in the garden, with his boat . . . the silver-framed wedding photos of Uncle Willie and Aunt Virginia, Grandma and Grandpa Bascome, but none of our mother and father . . . I longed to be back in our apartment when Daddy, Mummy, Nikki, and I were all together. The apartment was always ringing with voices. "Artists," Daddy would say, pulling me into his lap after the last guest had left, "are a very voluble and volatile group."

"And, quite often," our mother would add, looking up from her perch on the edge of the chair by Nikki, head bent, hunched over, pasting more of his beautiful photos into his album, "can be rather wearying."

These were the quiet times together for which Nikki and I waited. Shut up there together, all the guests gone. Everything was hushed and still and safe . . . Perhaps that is what Nikki had been trying to recapture in his world of silence.

On every visit to Brookhaven, the doctors assured us Nikki was progressing. And we must understand, they explained, Nikki truly did believe his mother had died a natural death. Albeit too young, too soon, but in her own room, in bed, or whatever the fantasy. He did not pretend to believe this, he actually believed it. He had blocked out the real truth because it was too painful for him to accept.

His loss of speech—they explained so simply—was because if he did not speak he would not have to talk about this painful experience. He might even, they suggested, have some feelings of guilt because he hadn't been able to save her, trapped as he was on the rocks above the lake, witnessing the whole tragedy and powerless to help. Whatever it might be he did not need to communicate any of his feelings if he couldn't speak.

So while Nikki struggled to regain his speech, I struggled to find myself, who I was, where I belonged. There was the agony of Miss Ridgely's Dance Classes where, having remained as Nella would describe me, *una piccolo raggazza*, I suffered the indignity of being dragged around the huge expanse of the Plaza ballroom by some tall, gangly youth who acted as though he'd been stuck with someone's baby sister. Often I'd sit on the edge of one of those spindly gold chairs that ringed the parquet floor in an agony of suspense, waiting for someone to ask me to dance or hoping to God they would not. Then, suddenly, on my seventeenth birthday, the paints arrived. A great untidy brown paper parcel with no card, nothing inside, only the return address, Brookhaven, to indicate from whom it had come. This began my first serious consideration of art as a career. I took my birthday check from Aunt Virginia and Uncle Willie and enrolled in the Art Students League. From the moment I heard the voices ringing through the corridors, saw the students, smelled the paint and fixative, felt the new canvases, the stick of charcoal between my fingers, I knew I'd found the place where I belonged.

Six months later, on a Sunday in May, I drove out to

Brookhaven with the beginnings of a portfolio. Nikki had graduated from the institution now and was living on his own in a small housekeeping apartment in the upper half of a little frame house on the main street of the village. This was a kind of test as to how he would manage in the world outside. He had begun to speak now, but we never, on any of our visits, spoke about the past, the villa, or our mother. It was as though he had shut the door on that part of his life—as indeed he had—and now looked only to the future. It was that shut door and what lay behind it that held his memory of our mother's death, and he would not unlock it. He would, the doctors insisted, in his own time, when he was ready. There was nothing more they could do for him. But just seeing any improvement made it a happy visit. Nikki had telephoned, and this was exciting enough in itself, as he still tended to avoid most verbal communications, preferring to write little notes or sometimes creating an amusing collage of old snaps to deliver his message. But he had telephoned to invite me to "a farewell dinner." I waited. You did not interrupt Nikki or you might lose him altogether. Finally he went on, "It's my farewell to Brookhaven. I've been formally discharged. I want you to come out for dinner. I'm cooking. Come at five and we'll dine when we're ready. Oh, and bring whatever pictures you have." He hung up. I packed every painting and sketch I had and lugged the portfolio over to Penn Station and caught the one-fifteen for Brookhaven. The single cabbie that served the village flipped his cap at me in greeting. He'd gotten to know us by now. Before I could direct him, he said, "Goin to Widder Martin's place this time . . . coulda walked there if ya didn't have that big carton with ya. No mind. Glad to drop ya." And he wouldn't let me even pay him. The Widow Martin's house was set back from a broad sweep of lawn on a tree-lined street in the heart of this village that had been incorporated in 1789. The car turned into the little narrow drive, overhung with lilac bushes, just as Nikki was clumping up the front porch in great rubber boots carrying a bushel basket of steamers. The cabbie hooted his horn to announce our arrival. Nikki set down the basket and called out, "Be right with you," and the words were like bright golden stars spilling out of the heavens at me. I watched as he sat on the weathered, sun-bleached steps leading to the front porch, pulling off his boots. By the time I dragged myself and the portfolio from the cab, he'd clumped off his boots, jumped the steps barefoot and swung me around in a great bear hug.

"C'mon"—picking up the basket of clams—"you can help." And he led me through the back door into the cool, old-fashioned kitchen. "Bring your portfolio?"

"You better believe it."

"Good." He handed me a glass of chilled wine. "Let's look at them."

"Now! I just got here."

"Well, you can relax . . . drink your wine . . . and I'll go over the pictures, O.K.?"

I slid down from the stool and went back outdoors past the raspberry bushes and the runner beans and lugged in the portfolio.

Nikki did not speak at all while he studied the pictures. He went over them several times, juggling and reassembling them in some kind of sequence which only he understood. He was enthusiastic about them, yet I had the feeling, all the while, that he was looking for something—some particular thing that would have special meaning or significance for him—or us. It was only a feeling I had. Nothing I could put my finger on. And besides, after months of exposure to the clinic at Brookhaven, one began to imagine one always looked for the hidden meaning behind everything. I put it out of my mind and when he'd finished with my pictures he brought out his portfolio and *his* passport!

"I decided," he said. "Or maybe I should say *we* decided. We're all very "We" orientated here, you know. We say things like 'The decision is entirely yours, Nikki,' and then we say, 'Well, let's look at the alternatives.'" Nikki laughed, and the sound was sweet and heartwarming. "So *we* made the decision and I am off to Paris and Tunis and then God knows where—" He took a stance in the middle of the room. Barefooted, bare-chested, jeans rolled to his knees, his sun-streaked hair tousled. You would not think he had been ill a day. But I did not have to think. I knew. Now he made a fist of each hand and cupping them to his eyes, pivoted in imitation of a camera zooming around the room. "The roving eye of Nikki Grazzi sees all, knows all." Then he flopped down on his tidy little studio couch, shuffling through the collection of glossies he'd collected in his portfolio. Almost all were familiar to me. I'd shared so much of his early picture taking. There was Sieppi working in the gardens, the thin line of yews marching along to the entrance of the villa, the mascara-eyed raccoon in close-up, the first snow of the season on top the Ramapos . . . while I studied them, I felt Nikki staring down at me, suddenly strangely quiet. When I looked up his expression never changed. It was as though a curtain had suddenly dropped between us. Or between Nikki and the rest of the world. I felt my heart begin to hammer and my fingers tightening on the pictures. What had gone wrong? Had anything been said or implied? The pictures scattered to the floor. "Oh, Nikki, I'm sorry . . . wait . . . I'll do it." I gathered them all up carefully, stacking them neatly one after the other like a deck of cards. "My, who's this?" And I picked up a picture of a slim, soigné female in cut-offs, hair in pigtails, stretched out across a sloop in the local harbor.

"Oh, her mother does the cleaning here . . . I thought she was kind of photogenic and she offered to let me shoot her."

"She is indeed photogenic. Y'know, if all else fails Nikki, you could become another Avedon, photographing high-fashion models."

"Perish the thought." He laughed. This seemed to help break the spell.

When the cabbie was back at the door and I was leaving to catch the train back to town, Nikki leaned in the doorway for a moment, and holding fast to my hand said:

"Don't worry, Franca. It's going to be all right." Then this serious face broke into smiles again and he said, "Look, I'll bring back a whole new world for you and we can try to recapture it together."

True to his word he had brought back a whole new world on film, and it was for everyone to share. He had "shot" his way around the world and the people and messages he brought back would speak through his pictures. His letters had been beautiful and vivid as I knew his photos would be. But the doctor's words echoed through my mind. "Sooner or later all in his good time he will work this through." But even that didn't matter now. What mattered was we were here, together once again. He had come home. . . .

CHAPTER FOUR

Now, as though suddenly springing from the earth, Villa Belsola came into sight. There in the vapory mists this replica of a fifteenth-century Italian estate loomed large and gray, the courtyard blackened with rain. Red crenelated roofs undulated over the main house, guest house, and gardener's cottage, and beyond to the stables and chapel. Tall pines rose up in the distance, then gave way to vast stretches of green and formal gardens, box hedges, waxen shrubs, and isolated topiary. I stared straight ahead.

I did not even want to glance in the direction of the chapel, now probably strangled with vines and ivy growing from its disuse. But once, as a child, I had explored it, and as I stood in the crypt drenched in rays of molten dust filtering through the tiny windows, the pungent stench of damp earth rising from the cold floors, the massive oak doors had suddenly slammed shut with a frightening finality, trapping me inside. I closed my eyes against the memory of that terror that threatened to overwhelm me now just as it had then. I had thrown myself against those doors till my arms and shoulders grew numb, screams locked inside so my lips moved soundlessly like a ventriloquist's dummy, until I fell against the wood like a cloth doll and watched through eyes blurred with tears as the sun gave way to night. The darkness pressed flat against the windows seeming to blot out everyone and everything I knew . . . leaving just the chapel and me, and noises and threats that seem to grow and prowl in the darkness. Then just as suddenly as the doors had shut, they opened and I was rescued by darling Sieppi. My tear-stained face pressed against the warmth of his chest while I took great gulping sobs as he crooned and tried to comfort me. Everyone was more "afraid" than I was, he had laughed . . . first combing the woods and lakes and then the chapel. The doors were locked from the outside, its heavy iron bolt slammed into place, and though we all pretended the wind had done it, there was the silent suggestion that Nikki, as a child's prank, had followed and locked me in. Then as most children who see their harmless joke blown to proportions beyond their understanding, he was afraid to speak.

I'd never said anything to him. For after all, it was he who pleaded I not go in and I never admitted how afraid I'd really been and then perhaps after all, it had been the wind.

I reached across the car to touch him, but feeling the perspiration on my hand, drew back.

"Nikki, remember old Sieppi?"

"The old gardener?" Nikki fingered his long hair and glistening sideburns. "Must have been about ninety when we first came here. Wore funny clothes all the time. He stayed on after Grandfather died, to work for Phelps, right?"

"Right! Only I don't think he really ever worked for

Phelps. I think he just stayed for Mummy's sake, wouldn't you say?"

"I'd say almost everyone did."

"Oh, Nikki." I'd never been too turned on by my stepfather but Nikki had a way of voicing things I never dared. I wondered why, then, if he really felt this way about Phelps, he'd been so insistent we come here.

I motioned at the back of the chauffeur's head. A glass partition separated us. I hoped it was soundproof. Nikki just winked at me.

"Well, maybe not everyone. But surely the staff. After all"—Nikki lapsed into an effete parody of a female voice —"Grandfather just *adored* Phelps—"

"Portrait of Aunt Virginia and very good, too. Well, let's say he certainly *approved* of Phelps."

"Which is more than he did our father, is that what you're saying?"

"Well, it's true, isn't it? I often felt Grandfather wished Mother had married Phelps right from the first."

"Like straight out of kindergarten or dancing class?"

We both fell back into silence then, broken only by the rhythm of the windshield wipers and the steady *hish* of tires, each of us caught up in our own memories of the villa.

The car swung into the wide circular courtyard and pulled up on the wet flagstone. I glanced at Nikki once, quickly, apprehensively. He looked so handsome leaning forward to hitch his camera gear over his shoulder. He wore an open-throated shirt under a tan corduroy jacket and blue jeans. He *looked* an artist.

I reached out my hand to him for reassurance. After all, it was he who'd insisted we accept our stepfather's rather strange summons to the villa. He squeezed my hand and smiled. Then his face settled into a kind of remote thoughtfulness, not at all the kind of look I associated with that fun-loving brother, the boy before the tragedy, who'd let me go trailing after him to catch "frenchies" in the big pond behind the stables or who would hoist me into any of the old gnarled trees that grew everywhere in the Park and catch me as I jumped. But it was going to take time. We'd been separated for so long—we had a lot of catching up to do.

Dudley, looking more than ever like a movie-stereotype butler, broke my reverie, stepping forward, now bracing himself against the driving winds and rain, struggling to open a large black umbrella. He sent a young houseboy in a white jacket around to help with the bags. Nikki, the collar of his jacket upturned, leaped from the car and tried to help, too. I followed more sedately, skipping puddles under the protection of the umbrella.

Once inside, shaking the drops of rain from us like puppy dogs, I turned to greet Dudley. Why, he'd hardly changed at all! His hair was as white as I remembered and he still carried himself erect. His long, egg-shaped face was only a little more lined, and his drooping eyes gave him the look of a rather overanxious Bassett hound. I half expected him to tousle my hair and pick me up in his arms as he did when I was a child. But he just clasped my hands in both of his. He seemed glad to see us, but that was more than could be said for Mrs. Dudley. She, too, looked just as I remembered her; the same dish face with the pug nose, her iron-gray hair not one bit whiter, and her eyes seemed deep-set, almost reptilian, the way the lids lowered like a turtle or a frog and the eyeballs swiveled about to take in everything.

The great, cavernous hall with the same massive armoire delicately traced with elaborate flowers and figurines was just as I remembered. The two Dante chairs guarded either side of the huge heraldic tapestry which even now swayed ever so slightly with the current of air rippling through the hall. I remembered how, as children racing through the corridor over the sleek terrazzo tiles, we thought it was just like the Metropolitan Museum where we often went with Daddy and Mummy. It even had the dank chill of cold, sweating stone and the hush of a museum about it.

But for me, everything about this place was touched with tragedy. For both of us. I wanted to run. Instead I reached over and pretending to fasten the leather straps of my sandals, wet and slimy from the rain, lurched against Nikki and whispered:

"I'm scared of this place, Nikki. It really gives me the creeps."

He acted as though he hadn't heard, but I knew when I saw the nerve in his cheek begin to twitch that he had. He appeared enormously concerned with the maneuvering of the luggage. Then he smiled broadly, too, took hold of my hand and led me toward the wide stone stairway where, as children, we had so often huddled together. We followed

Mrs. Dudley, the luggage, and the houseboy up to our rooms.

"You're just overlooking the lake, Master Nikki," Mrs. Dudley told him, smoothing down the gold twill bedspread in typically housekeeper fashion. Then she pulled back the drapes. I jumped as a gust of rain rattled against the pane. I felt that tightening in the pit of my stomach again and the feeling I must hold my breath until I burst. But Nikki was testing the bed, bouncing up and down on it once or twice, and said, "Ah, so I see. Mmh, this is a first-rate bed."

He moved restlessly about the room, tugging at books, opening bureau drawers, looking in closets. Mrs. Dudley stood by all the while her hands folded across her middle, her rigidly tasteful blue afternoon dress with its below-calf hemline looking curiously antiquated. The obsidian glitter of her eyes took in every move.

"That'll be locked tight," she volunteered as Nikki tugged at a door, "we've put in another bath just here, d'ya see." She moved toward the other end of the room.

"Oh, Nikki, wasn't that—" He silenced me with a look. If Mrs. Dudley noticed I'd stopped in mid-sentence, she gave no indication. Very probably she was quite aware I'd intended to remind Nikki that behind the door was a bathroom once promised him to be converted into his very own darkroom. There he was going to be able to develop his own prints. It had been his boyhood dream. But after our mother's death, nothing ever came of his dream room with rows and rows of enamel trays filled with developing fluids and all the negatives strung across the room to dry on wires held fast with tiny pins.

But that didn't matter, I thought, looking at him with all the tenderness I felt for him rising in my throat. He's made it without that. He had captured in his photos what I hoped I could in my drawings.

"When you've had a wash-up, perhaps you'd wish to join Mr. and Mrs. Trent in the small sitting room for cocktails?"

"Oh, Aunt Virginia and Uncle Willie are here?"

"Yes, miss. And I'm to make apologies for your stepfather. Mr. Warton is not quite up to joining you this evening. He has asked me to make his excuses. I'm sure he'll be more himself by tomorrow." Her small speech delivered, Mrs. Dudley held the door waiting for me to precede her. I held back.

"Thank you," I told her, curling one spear of hair self-consciously behind my ear, "Nikki will help me unpack."

"Very good, miss. You're to be in the special guest room—you'll recall?"

She sounded to me like—small matter to me who helps you with your luggage. What a nasty woman she was. I loathed her. The feeling, I was sure was mutual. Oh, why had we ever come back to this hateful, unhappy place?

"Listen, Nikki," I said when Mrs. Dudley had shut the door behind her and he, in wild pantomime of "I Spy," had rushed to fling it open, hoping to catch her in an ear-to-keyhole act. "Whatever possessed you to have us come back here? Did you suppose the old man intended to do right by us on his deathbed? Supposing, of course, he *is* on his deathbed. And what kind of a family gathering can he have in mind? He obviously invited Willie and Virginia as well."

"Franca, dear, relax," Nikki put his arm around me and nudged me toward the door, dragging my bags with him.

I forged into the guest room ahead of Nikki.

"Put them anywhere," I told him as he struggled with a luggage rack.

I moved around the room gingerly. I remembered it perfectly, and it was, indeed, our mother's special guest room. It was as though the room waited, as it had when our mother was alive, for her next favored guest.

The almost almond-pale fruitwood Florentine bed with its wreaths of delicate pastel fruits and flowers dominated the room. The pale blue brocade canopy hung above the headboard rippling down in a sweeping panel to the floor below. The walls were done in matching blue brocade and in direct line of vision from the bed hung the Madonna of the Consolation by Biagio.

I closed my eyes and saw my mother, her paint brush clenched between her teeth as she stood off, head to one side, eyes squinting, studying her work, saying, "This Biagio not to be confused with one Bernadino Biagio often called Pinturicchio—'the little painter'—"

"Or called Sordichio, sometimes, because he was deaf and kind of plumpy," I would interrupt with great glee.

"Right." Mummy would take the brush from between her lips and lean over to kiss me. She always smelled deliciously of her perfume, Caron's Bellodgia, and oil paints and turpentine.

"Me too, me too." Nikki would fling himself on her.

"Oh, my darlings, I love you!" She would fall on her knees beside us, embracing us both in her arms, rocking back and forth, hugging us. Then she would become very quiet and we knew she was remembering our father and all the past happiness. The one great void, no matter how much we loved her, we could not fill . . .

"Penny for 'em, Francesca—to coin a phrase."

"Just thinking," I stepped out of my wet sandals.

"Don't, that's a bad business."

"What, going barefoot or thinking?"

"Thinking. Look, I'll wait for you. When you're ready, knock, and we'll go down together." Nikki flipped open the locks of my bag and I was somehow relieved and comforted to see my familiar worn terry scuffs, my cotton pajamas, and my little watered-silk make-up kit.

"Keep the faith, baby," he said, and walked out.

I took my toilet kit into the dressing room, dumped its contents out on the dressing table, and started to run my bath. Above me on a small rack were rows and rows of toothbrushes in their cellophane coffins. Alongside, still in their colorful wrappings, were soaps from Morny, Bendel, or Bergdorf's; facial tissues and creams; cleansing, nutritive, daytime, nighttime, dry skin, oily skin; from Elizabeth Arden to Estee Lauder. I realized I would have traveled quite comfortably with only my navy canvas tote bag. But my own beat-up make-up brush and mascara and half-emptied jar of cream seemed suddenly oneself in an alien atmosphere. For although Nikki and I had spent many years in this house, there was always something alien about it.

Rain continued to drip from the eaves and gurgle down the drain pipes. Wind battered tree branches against the tall windows where the long brocade curtains remained quite impervious to the summer storm that raged outside.

I drew a huge monogrammed towel—thirsty, the advertising copywriters call them—from its warming rod, stepped out of my clothes and into a warm jasmine-scented tub.

I lay soaking in this warm, luxurious bath thinking what memories this house must hold for us all. I was grateful to have Nikki back with me. Grateful we were now finally together.

Lying there luxuriating in this tub I must have dozed off. I came awake suddenly, my heart thudding the way it does when in a dream one stumbles or falls from the edge of sleep—waking with a start. But I hadn't actually been asleep. I'd been daydreaming. I ran a face cloth under icy water and buried my face in it. I had been daydreaming about this house, wondering why I'd been given this room where, if I stood on tiptoe as a child, I could clearly see the golden dome of the chapel. And why had Nikki been given the room overlooking the lake—when his one visit here, even under the guidance of Brookhaven doctors, had been so disastrous, they thought he might never speak again.

Why . . . ? Why . . . ? And, why had we even been invited—summoned was more like it—back to Villa Belsola?

CHAPTER FIVE

When Nikki knocked, I'd finished dressing and was standing at the window thinking again this room must have been chosen deliberately. No one else had this fear of that ancient chapel now long overgrown with tangled ivy and leaves, birds' nests tucked under the eaves. Sometimes in my dreams I used to fancy I heard the sound of the great rush of wings when something—I never knew what—frightened the birds and they'd fan out wildly into the air as though some demon or great bird of prey pursued them. I shuddered at the thought of it. I'd often wondered why our Grandfather Bascome, patently so anti-papist, hadn't had the original owners of Villa Belsola, who had special dispensation for Mass to be heard there, raze the building before he'd bought the estate. Obviously someone must have conned him into believing it was wildly romantic, all part of the scene. Or, at the very least, a conversation piece.

I stood there half dreaming, again seeing and yet not seeing through the haze and rain that continued to fall, when there appeared to be someone moving out there by the chapel gates. I'd still have to stand on tiptoe, I thought ruefully, if I wanted to get a full view and be certain someone actually was moving through that misting rain. The summer lightning illuminated the sky momentarily silhouetting a figure in a bright red plaid raincoat. It was just then Nikki knocked.

"You look charming, Miss Grazzi," Nikki said. "What say we go down and join the rest of our devoted family—what's left of it."

I looked up quickly. I hated to hear that thin edge of acerbity in Nikki's voice and a tone which had never been there before. But then I had to keep reminding myself he had been through so much. I could not possibly hope he would remain that golden-haired boy I had once known; although there were, happily, always glimpses of him.

"I hardly remember Phelps at all, Nikki . . . or do I tell myself I don't remember him because I don't wish to remember him?"

"Stay tuned to this station and you will receive more sage advice from Dr. Rose Franzblau . . . if *you* have a problem you would like to discuss, stay tuned . . ."

"You idiot!" I laughed. "Shut up."

"I like you, too." Nikki put his arm around me. "Shall we go down now?" He released me for a moment then went to the mirror to straighten his tie. I turned back to the window. There *was* someone there. I hadn't been deceived by haze and misting rain. But then anyone had a perfect right to be walking out there if they wished. Only who would choose such a night for a constitutional? It was certainly rather odd to be walking out there in the rain. Unless, of course, a clandestine meeting . . . lovers meeting . . . ? Here, at this isolated villa? Highly unlikely. Even I could see how absurd that was, although certainly there had been something rather clandestine about the whole thing . . . I'd had the distinct impression of *two* someones out there.

"Nikki." I tugged at his arm. "Come here a minute will you?"

We stood together at the window.

"Dreary, isn't it?" he said.

"Nikki, wait."

"Franca, what's the matter?"

But there was no one out there.

"Look, Nikki, don't think I've flipped, but there was someone—two someones, I think—down there just now."

"Down where?"

"There. Out there."

He peered close to the glass. "I don't see anyone now. Besides, what's wrong with that? No law about walking around in the rain. Do it all the time in the city, don't we? I mean, what's the difference?"

"Mmmh, I suppose, only this is so isolated here. And we're all together. Who could it be? I mean, who would be wandering around this property we wouldn't know about?"

"Whoa . . . just a minute . . ." Nikki put his arm around me again. I shivered involuntarily. I felt my skin crawl, the way, we used to say, when someone is walking on your grave.

"Franca, baby, how do we know we don't know whoever it might be out there . . . I mean there might be new staff—not only Boots, the houseboy, for instance. And for all we know, there could be other guests any or all of whom could have a perfect right to be walking around out there." He hugged me closer for a moment. "Y'know, I think you've just got some kind of hang-up about that chapel business."

"Yes, maybe, but—"

If I had been going to say more about my misgivings regarding the figures I'd seen out there, I was interrupted by the arrival of Mrs. Dudley, who knocked once, then entered.

"There is nothing," Nikki said under his breath to me, "like waiting to be asked in, huh? Ah, Mrs. Dudley," he said affably, "we were just coming down."

"Mrs. Trent said she'd be pleased to meet you in the small sitting room for cocktails whenever you are ready."

As we followed Mrs. Dudley out the door, I wondered if this had been in the nature of a command to appear on schedule . . . her, Mrs. Dudley's schedule . . . so that dinner or whatever could go off on time, her time. She'd been like that as long as I remembered her.

The gold draperies had been drawn and a small fire lit in the sitting room to take out the summer damp. The cocktail things were set out. I sat down in the nearest little gold brocade chair while Nikki, seemingly more at ease, walked over to the stereo and began riffling through records.

"Mrs. Trent will be down directly. It's nice to have you both back." I marveled at the silent tread that had led Dudley into the sitting room across the marble tiles without being heard. "I don't know what might be of interest to you, Mr. Nikki, but you're welcome to play whatever suits your fancy. May I . . . ?" And Dudley maneuvered his way around the stereo, fiddling with knobs and setting the volume. As he bent down, I became aware of glistening drops of water on his hair, highlighted now under the lamp and a dark stain of dampness that spread across his shoulders. Dudley . . . out there . . . by the chapel? It could have been. But before I could pursue this line of thought the familiar strains of an oldie, "Smoke Gets in Your Eyes," softly filled the sitting room and Dudley was gone as silently as he'd arrived.

The fire gave a pleasant, convivial glow to the room. It was always referred to as the small sitting room and was always, for as long as memory, that place where everyone gathered for before-dinner drinks. Done in formal gold brocade there was, nevertheless, a special warmth to this room probably because of the contemporary note lent by the stereo and TV, although both were hidden behind fine-grain paneling. And most of all because of the bright-colored and arresting oils Mummy had done of the gardens and the lily pond out back. Although she was, as she'd declared herself, a dilettante, it was evident whatever artistic ability Nikki or I had came from our mother's side of the family.

The two outer walls were lined with shelves tumbling books, many of them old fiction dating back to the thirties and most of them without their dust jackets. The whole area had a comfortably disordered look about it that was appealing and the aura of our mother's personality hung over the room everywhere. Over the fireplace, dominating the room, was the portrait of our mother seated on the grass in the garden, wearing the pale yellow frock, cradling Biscuit, her cairn terrier, in her arms, a large-brimmed straw hat idly tossed aside lying on the ground nearby and sunshine seeping through the leaves to light her already beautiful and luminous face.

"Ah, Francesca, my dear. . . ."

I swung around. "Aunt Virginia . . . Uncle Willie. . . ." I moved across the room and embraced them each automatically, planting a light kiss on their cheeks.

"Good to see you, good to see you," Uncle Willie said to no one in particular. "Ah, Dudley, thank you." Dudley had arrived with the ice. "Shall I?" Willie asked. "By all means, sir." Nikki's manner seemed falsely deferential. Or perhaps it was because I had not seen him in just such a situation before.

"Whiskey and water for me, please." Then, turning to me, Nikki asked, "The usual, Fran?"

"Yes, please, and Plymouth gin if you have it. Straight up with a twist of lemon."

Dinner seemed stilted and awkward. Dudley, with a change of jacket, served, walking around the table with his long, egg-shaped face sadly solemn, almost funereal. Mummy used to say dining at the villa was rather like dining in the Sistine Chapel. Cherubim and seraphim floated in diaphanous trails of delicately pastel paints across the ceiling, flecked with bits of antique gold. The side panels were magnificent loggias and villas, vineyards and the Adriatic stretching away, the best example of trompe l'oeil, so if conversation waned one could always throw oneself into the artist's mood and float away to foreign scenes. This made the Scottish Dudleys even more incongruous in this household. The whole thing seemed of another time and place.

Virginia was in the inevitable little black number—this one a silk matte jersey—and loops of pearls making a bib at the neck, and although Willie wasn't in black tie the whole effect was one of somber formality.

We had icy wedges of melon wrapped in prosciutto ham to start, and with the first course, Virginia asked politely about Nikki's work.

"How is the painting coming along, Nikki? Oh no, foolish woman," she chastised herself, "it's photography, isn't it?"

"Yes, Aunt Virginia, it's photography."

Virginia sat back and sipped her chablis. She had done her share. Willie cleared his throat and asked how Nikki enjoyed being back in civilization.

"Darling," Virginia addressed herself to me over Willie and Nikki's conversation, "tell me how you are managing in your little apartment? Are you eating properly? Is it safe? Have you a steady beau? We do miss you, don't we Willie. Willie . . ."

Dudley was clearing and Willie was rescued momentarily.

"You know, Nikki, Willie and I never really wanted Francesca to leave us and—"

Willie dismissed the subject with a wave of his hand. "I'm sure Francesca has always been well aware of how we feel about her, Virginia."

I felt suddenly guilty somehow, as though I hadn't properly performed the litany of how grateful I was to them, how much I missed them.

The poached salmon took us through my sketch classes at the League and then into Nikki's show.

"Oh dear, I do hope they're not all those dreadfully depressing pictures of starving natives and that sort of thing."

Nikki remained noncommittal and totally indifferent, which I realized could pass for a kind of modesty.

"They're really rather like Raghu Rai's work, if you ask me."

Nikki lifted his glass to me, "I take that as the ultimate compliment."

Virginia looked to Willie, her glazed blue eyes querying him as to who in the world Raghu Rai might be . . . Ah, well . . .

This got us through the main course. A delicious chocolate soufflé followed, and coffee, it appeared, was to be served back in the sitting room.

Coffee and liqueurs were set out on the long table against the far wall. "Virginia?" Willie held a small cup aloft.

"Not for me, I find it much too stimulating at this hour."

"Franca?"

"Oh yes, please . . . but would you like me to do the serving, Uncle Willie?" I half rose to go toward him, when Dudley suddenly appeared. "Ah, Dudley." Uncle Willie turned. "I was just going to ask if we could have some lemon peel." I sank back into my seat. Willie obviously enjoyed this.

"Right here, sir."

Uncle Willie shook his head. "Dudley, you never miss anything."

"I hope not, sir." Then, addressing the room, "May I serve anyone a liqueur, brandy? Mr. Warton requested I put the liqueurs at your disposal."

"How is he, Dudley?" Aunt Virginia asked.

"Better I should think, madam. I expect he'll be joining you all in the morning." He hesitated a moment. "I think he was disappointed not to be with you, to welcome you all this evening."

"Well, I'm glad he is feeling better. Thank you, Dudley."

At the door Dudley paused. "Mrs. Dudley asked if anyone wishes a tray for breakfast; otherwise, breakfast will be served at nine."

"Good heavens, no. At least not for me," I said, thinking how I squeezed orange juice, standing at the refrigerator door, tossed the skins in the trash while I waited for the toast to pop, and poured tea with the other hand, while I scanned the New York *Times* headlines.

Virginia thought she might like a tray, while Willie said he'd be down. This achieved, Dudley bid us good night.

The rain continued to beat against the pane, the fire spit once or twice, then, "Smoke Gets in Your Eyes" came to its melodic end. Looking down from that happy moment in the garden, captured forever on canvas was our mother. Suddenly the silence was broken by a tapping sound above us, coming from somewhere upstairs. We sat fixed, waiting for the sound to stop. It didn't. Finally Uncle Willie said, "What on earth is that?"

"What is what, Willie?"

"That pounding sound, Virginia, the pounding noise?"

"Oh, *that*," she said. We waited.

"Well?"

She looked from one to the other of us in embarrassment.

"Goodness, *I* don't know."

"Well, the way you said, 'Oh, *that*,' we naturally assumed you did know, Virginia."

"Well, sorry to disappoint you, Willie, but I don't."

"Hush . . ." Nikki held up his hand for silence. "Listen."

We listened.

"Sounds like a doorknob rattling," I said.

"I think, child, what you mean to convey is the sound of someone rattling a doorknob."

"Whatever it is, it's stopped now."

Indeed it had, and now there was the sound of a door banging shut and something being pulled or dragged across the floor. Then silence.

"Well, shall we retire?" Willie chugged his drink.

Whether it was the fire and sudden warmth or the good food and good wine, I began suddenly to feel incredibly sleepy. I could hardly keep awake.

"C'mon, Fran—we're just down the hall from each other," he explained to Aunt Virginia.

"Yes, dear, I know. Well, good night."

I yawned. "Oops, forgive me." Virginia came and put her arm around me.

"It's been a very emotional day for you, I'm sure. No wonder you're exhausted. Do try and get a good night's sleep."

We made our way carefully up the stairs and along the dimly lit corridor. Just as we reached Nikki's room we heard the tapping beginning again—lightly, but unmistakably. We froze. "It's coming from there," Nikki said and edged toward the door at the end of the corridor. We crept quietly along the hall and were almost in reach of the massive, carved oak door when Dudley appeared from the servants' wing. We both stopped still like two children caught in some minor infraction of household law.

"We—there was a funny sound—we wondered if anything was wrong," my voice trailed off feebly.

"Nothing is wrong, miss."

"But that noise . . . ?"

"What noise?"

Nikki persisted, "It was a kind of hammering noise. We all heard it. We heard it downstairs having coffee."

"Oh . . . oh, I see." Dudley seemed to study us for a moment. "Well, I daresay it's Mr. Warton. He sometimes forgets, you know."

"Forgets?"

"Yes, he forgets he has a bellpull. Right alongside his bed in fact. He need only ring. He probably wants to retire and it's an ordeal . . . he can't quite manage alone. I'll get Boots and we'll get him into bed."

"Can we help?" I asked awkwardly.

"I think not, miss, thank you. If there is nothing further I can do for you I'll bid you good night."

Dudley turned and walked off down the hall. It was obvious he intended we should do the same. Nikki waited. He waited until Dudley was out of sight, then went to the great oak door and leaned against it, turning the knob. It was locked. There was no further sound from inside.

"Nikki, c'mon. Let's get to bed before Dudley comes back."

Nikki felt along the sides of the door, tried the knob again, then gave up.

I was so tired I did not even remember getting into bed.

CHAPTER SIX

My sleep was restless. I tossed and turned, pummeling my pillow first into one shape then another, then flung my arms out where they struck the brocade panels of the canopy, which seemed to cut off whatever air managed to circulate through the room on this humid summer night. Somehow, then, I was back at the chapel door, the currents of wind filtering through the tentacles of ivy that clung to the building making little sucking noises. "That's the dead people breathing in there, trying to get out," the children would say, spooking themselves and running away screaming in a kind of joyous terror. After all they didn't live in the shadow of that chapel as we did. It was more for fun and games for them. But Nikki and I lived here. We belonged—in a way, at least, we belonged—and certainly the chapel was ours. I remember how, even then, Nikki was always more sensitive than the other children. It was Nikki who knew all the wildlife that inhabited the Park and surrounding woodlands. Nikki, who could not bear to hurt a living thing, who once bravely rescued a raccoon from the steel trap, its tiny paw crushed and bleeding, then promptly fainted dead away. I think it was the horror of that sound in the chapel that haunted Nikki and me. I was determined to prove it was ridiculous. They'd just been trying to scare us. We knew, "When you're dead you're dead . . . there's no such things as ghosts . . . and that's that. C'mon, Nikki, I'll prove it. That's only the wind . . . or maybe even some of your little woodland friends; chipmunks, field mice . . . its got to be a real thing, Nikki. There just aren't any ghosts, that's silly." But Nikki clung to my hand. "Please don't. Please don't go in there, Franca. I believe you. Honestly, I believe you. You don't have to prove it." But I had to prove it. I had to prove it to myself. I simply could not live with the boys. Richie De Meyer or his cousin Phillip Hamilton taunting us about some curse put upon us for neglecting the chapel. So I waited for a day when I thought Nikki was off somewhere exploring with his camera and bravely—bravely? —with hammering heart picked my way through the overgrown brush surrounding the chapel, threading through the tangled vines that laced and interlaced the stone steps leading down to the crypt. My mouth dried with fear and I remembered looking backward over my shoulder to see that no one, none of my tormentors were near so they might witness my fear as I plunged doggedly ahead and into the chapel . . . it was all there as real as the day it happened, something, a furry something—a rat? . . . My God, I hoped not—slithered across my foot and the cobwebs thick as Spanish moss clung to my face and feathery-light, dusty webs sucked into my nostrils, gagging me. Something like a shroud came down over my head and I screamed. I screamed again and again and again. Over and over and over and over . . . I sat bolt upright in bed, trembling in the dark. The panel of silken brocade wrapped around my face. I felt a moth. I beat and tore at the brocade panel with my hands as though it were a living thing with a mind of its own bent on destroying me. I rolled to the floor, flaying at the curtain, and crawled in the darkness toward the light switch, sobbing. Where was I? I couldn't remember. Suddenly the room sprang into light and someone was there, standing in the doorway. "Oh God"—I pulled myself up, staggering a little under the folds of the canopy still wrapping itself around my body. I leaned against the wall for support.

"Francesca . . . what on earth . . . ?"

"Oh, Aunt Virginia . . . oh, God . . . it's you. Thank God." I held out my hand toward her, I could not stop the trembling.

"My goodness, child, you must have waked the whole household." I could see behind her now, through the opened door, to Dudley's solemn face above his flannel robe held clutched at his throat. His long, skinny legs looking curiously incongruous trailing down under his short nightshirt. Mrs. Dudley was close behind him. Her thin, gray rattail braid swinging over her shoulder.

"Nikki? Where's Nikki?" I was still quivering, my legs threatening to give out under me any moment.

"He must be in his room, dear, although how he could still be asleep is beyond me. Your screams were enough to wake the dead."

"Oh." I sank down into a little satin slipper chair.

"Did I really scream? I thought I imagined the scream . . . in my dream." I put my hand to my head. My temples were pounding.

"You must have had a horrible nightmare. Would you like a cup of warm milk and an aspirin, or a drop of brandy? I'm sure Dudley would get it for you." Virginia was properly solicitous, tucking the folds of her sprigged challis robe more carefully around her.

"No, no, nothing, thank you."

I wished Nikki was here, but I was too ashamed to say it after waking this entire household. "No," I said, moving toward the bed now, "I'll be fine. I'll just get a glass of water and go back to bed. I'm awfully sorry," I said to the covey of people standing in the doorway. "I'm really awfully sorry I disturbed everyone."

"That's all right, dear," Virginia came into the room, shutting the door on the Dudleys' retreating figures. "Is there anything I can get for you before I return to bed . . ."

I shook my head, feeling as though a vise were squeezing the back of my head; my mouth was oddly dry and parched. I could hardly manage to get my tongue around the words I struggled to say.

"You better go back to Uncle Willie."

"Very well. Goodness, how that brother of yours and Willie could have slept through this commotion I can't imagine. Well, they certainly must have very clear consciences, that's all I can say! Good night, dear, try and get some rest now." She switched off the light and went out, shutting the door quietly behind her.

I lay back and pressed my fingertips against my pulsing temples. Could a nightmare really have done this to me? My head throbbed, my mouth was parched with the sour taste of a hangover. But I'd hardly had anything to drink to speak of. The pain over my eyes was agonizing. It reminded me of that time I'd been heavily sedated after a skiing fall . . . yes, that's what it was like . . . like being drugged. No nightmare could have had such a lasting effect. A temporary panic with a sick headache, even a parched throat from panic but it would have disappeared. Just in the way it had when I was originally trapped in that chapel. I threw back the covers and climbed out of bed. I went into the bathroom and flipped on the light so it would illuminate some of the bedroom. I ran water for a drink, the glass chattering against the faucet in my trembling hand. Then staring into the mirror, I saw a faint dusty smudge across my cheek. I put up my hand and touched my face, tightening my teeth in a tremor of revulsion as the dusty fluff of cobweb came off my fingertips. I steeled myself against the sickening sensation of bile rising in my throat. I rinsed out my mouth with clear water and then padded quietly back into the bedroom. I flopped down on the bed. I wished I might have put on the bedroom light but I didn't want to needlessly attract any more attention to myself. I ran the tips of my fingers along the interior of the canopy and shuddered as the dusty webs rolled into threads along my fingers. My head continued to pound. Someone, some person, had been in this room tonight. And, the only way they could have come in and so attempted to terrorize me was if I had been drugged. Drugged? That sounded so bizarre, so dramatic, the kind of thing I could imagine on the Late Show with Lon Chaney. But I knew, by the feeling in my throat and the sick ache in my head and the fact someone had been able to enter this room without waking me could only mean something had knocked me out. I tried with the pulsing in my head to think what could have been given me and by whom. And the opportunity. Certainly it was not at cocktail time. I should never have been able to get through dinner. Coffee? The espresso? I could hear Virginia saying, "I find it too stimulating this time of night." Willie, Nikki at the coffee service . . . pouring, making after-dinner drinks, "How about you, Franca?" Willie asking me about lemon . . . I put my hand over my eyes to shut out this room and recreate the scene in the sitting room. Nikki asked . . . But who poured? . . . Willie had served me. Willie had asked Dudley for the lemon . . . and Willie had twisted it and dropped it in my cup. Anything else? It would only have been Willie. Virginia never came near the coffee. It certainly could not have been Nikki. Or perhaps Nikki and Willie had been drugged as well. Anyhow, I accepted the reality of a drug. Maybe that's why they hadn't appeared when I'd screamed.

 I dropped to my knees now and palms spread, felt carefully along the rug, feeling a little foolish—trembling with apprehension, searching for some sign that someone had indeed been in my room. Then, close to the head of my bed there were damp imprints. Someone who had recently been in the rain had stood there close to the head of my bed and terrorized me. And, very probably had earlier drugged the coffee. But who? And above all, why?

CHAPTER SEVEN

"This," I sighed, slouching lower on the seat alongside Nikki, "is the life, man. Wait till Dino sees this."

This referred to the small car which Gretz had brought around to the side of the terrace while we were lunching, with the polite but cryptic message that Mr. Warton had said we were to use this to drive into town, and added that Mrs. Dudley had asked would we be returning for dinner and what time. Very obviously she would have to plan the meal around us. Our stepfather was generous enough to give his blessing to our return to the city for Nikki's show in the person of this gorgeous, low-slung crimson Jaguar. This domestic trivia attended to, Nikki and I started off for the city. Safely ensconced in the front seat, the rain having let up long enough to savor the joys of riding through city streets in an open car, I almost felt giddy. Almost, because last night's nightmare still tugged at my consciousness, and except . . .

"Except doesn't it seem rather odd, to make the understatement of the year, that we've raced up here in a kind of command performance, have been wined and dined and even been loaned this scrumptious car for our trip into town but have not had sight or sign of our host who, incidentally, I might remind you is also our step-papa. Odd, wouldn't you say?"

"Mmh," Nikki was busy maneuvering the car through midtown traffic.

"Oh, come on, Nikki. You aren't even paying attention. And I think you should. Remember it was your idea we go up there . . . and I tell you the place gives me the creeps. Did you ever consider how much this resembles *Ten Little Indians* . . . ?"

"Now wait a minute. I must have missed a few of the murders."

"None yet. But I have the feeling if you wait around long enough, even that could happen! No, seriously, what I did mean was that kind of complete service . . . all our physical needs and appetites cared for by a non-appearing host. And why isn't he appearing? He's the one who asked us to come up, and you're the one insisted we do. If he doesn't show pretty soon, I'm for giving up and going home." I crossed my arms in resignation.

"No. Let's not do that. At least not just yet. Look, let's forget it for now—let's just concentrate on the show and try and enjoy it. Then, when we get back, if we don't get to see him, I'll send a note and tell him we're leaving, as obviously he doesn't intend to meet with us, O.K.?"

"O.K." I agreed. And now that we had some real plan of action I could sit back and enjoy the day. At least for a little while I would leave behind all the unhappiness and brooding misery of the villa and try and blot my foolish suspicions about being drugged from my mind. I began to feel a real exhilaration now at being back in town. I picked up our conversation at a more pleasant juncture. "I can't wait to see what Dino says when he sees this."

Nikki was amused. He assured me Dino wouldn't be in the least impressed and quite likely would assume someone had got us a "hot car." So many of Dino's friends and clients were moneyed, bored young executives that indeed a Jaguar would be quite commonplace. However, that didn't dampen my glee as I rode through town in this gorgeous car wearing my dirty blue jeans, body shirt, and bare feet thrust into bright yellow clogs.

As we turned into Tenth Street, that still rather elegantly residential street between Fifth and Sixth, there were already two Mercedeses and a white Cadillac parked in the tow-away zone adjacent to Dino's studio, confirming Nikki's reaction.

The white Cadillac, I guessed, would belong to the agent Dino was so anxious for Nikki to meet. He could sell Nikki's photos to a national magazine or certainly work up a book for him. Darling Dino, nothing was too much trouble for his friends. And how incongruous his house appeared in the middle of a tree-lined street sprung straight out of Henry James. True, the street began to deteriorate just where Dino's lavender and fuchsia house projected into the avenue. The house, which at one time had been an ordinary genteel boardinghouse with four stone steps, iron handrails either side leading up to the entrance, had been painted lavender with fuchsia and the steps led to a door on which his signature was scrawled in bright purple letters. It appeared at first sight to be a restaurant or shop. But the neighbors understood it was Dino's home, and as an artist and decorator he used it as a showcase for his work or those of his friends. There had been some consternation the morning the ladders were flung against the building and the house was suddenly splashed with this bizarre paint. Until then all the houses on this street were similar with brass trim kept highly polished and brass name plates at each door. The tiny patch of green, fenced in, outside each house was carefully tended, and the curved ailanthus tree was kept trimmed, bending against clear, sparkling windows. Inside you knew everything smelled of lemon wax furniture polish, furniture shone, and footsteps would be muffled by heavy taupe carpeting. Of course, the moment Sidney Schaltz, the movie producer, and his wife, moved into her father's house on this street, residents knew a change was coming. Dino climaxed this. But he'd managed to win over all his neighbors, who would stop, when they were dog-walking, to chat and admire his three poodles all of whom had their names neatly lettered across their pink iridescent collars.

So, except for Dino's house and the new deli that had opened at the end of the block, it was rather like a street out of another time. I could visualize Jamesian children here—all grown up and long gone now—rolling hoops in their high-button shoes and smocks, wearing round sailor hats or tam-o'-shanters. They would be quiet and obedient children and, in the evenings, they would play their latest piano pieces, "Für Élise" or "Rustle of Spring," while Papa sat over his evening coffee . . . all long gone now. . . .

"Coming, Franca?"

"You bet." I broke abruptly with the past, leaping from

the car with such exuberance my clog went flying but Nikki caught it in mid-air and slipped it back on my foot and we proceeded more sedately now, up the steps to the studio.

Whitewashed walls stretched away back toward the center rooms. Even the whitewash, however, and some delicate oriental scent could not disguise the odor of mildew and mice dirt that permeated the halls. At the end of a tunnel-like entrance sparsely spaced with great green plants, we heard a piano and guitar vying with a vocalist to see who could "Up, Up and Away" first . . . A girl in black leotards, misshapen green sweater, and flowing locks caught back in an untidy ponytail walked up to us with the splay-footed walk of some ballerinas and said:

"Hi, I'm Betty Jean, you must be Nikki and you're—"

"Fran, his sister," I put out my hand. "Thanks a million, Betty Jean. You were so great to do all the work. We really appreciate it."

"No sweat. It was fun. You wanna' fix your face or something?" She smiled, showing large, white, even teeth in a sallow face. A thin, dark line of fuzz ran along her upper lip. She wore no lipstick and only her eyes were made up—large, dark, melancholy eyes like one of the Keene children. We followed her carefully between two youths sprawled out on cushions, one of whom lifted his knees to let us pass, the other engrossed in his drink and the music, let us pick our way between his legs. She stopped at a bright orange monkscloth drape cutting off one part of the room. The curtain slid back on wooden rings with a great clatter and a couple leaped from an embrace on a black corduroy-covered bed.

"Oh, for God's sake, I thought you two had gone."

The girl on the bed tucked her blue workshirt into her jeans and combed her fingers through her Dutch-boy bob, grinning up at us. "This is Fran, Nikki's sister. This is Jennie and—"

"Would you believe Mr. Livingston," her escort smiled.

"How do you do—Mr. Livingston, I presume," I said.

"Nice to meet you."

Jennie was still rather dazed-looking, wearing a smeared mouth of some glistening lip rouge. She adjusted her granny glasses, tilted her head back, and said, "This is fab. I mean far out. I adore Nikki. I mean everyone does, right?" The youth glared at her in mock rage and combed his fingers through *his* Dutch bob.

"I mean his work, man." She whined defensively.

"I'm afraid I have to agree. But then I'm a bit prejudiced. Right, Nikki?" I turned to Nikki in time to see his legs disappear up the stairs, toward the exhibit.

"What," a voice behind me said, "is your special prejudice, if I may ask?" I turned and almost collided with the speaker who thrust a glass at me and said, "I'm Joe and this is gin, O.K.?"

"Hello, Joe, and gin is fine, thank you."

We moved in unison toward the stairs. At the foot of the stairway where a small knot of people were edging toward the studio, I looked at him. There was really nothing about him to distinguish him from the rest of this younger crowd. He wore the conventional workshirt and blue jeans and I noticed fringed moccasins. I noticed something else, too, that amused me. This was his mustache, so like Nikki's, it glinted with golden lights while his hair and eyebrows were almost black. Obviously, he must have been a blond baby!

He really looked the part, but there was something about him when I looked him straight in the eye as I was doing now while we clinked glasses, that gave me the feeling this was all so much camp for him. And he wasn't *that* young. Certainly, not quite as young as Nikki or me. I sensed he was play-acting. But he wasn't taking all this or himself so seriously. That was something in his favor.

"Seen the exhibition yet?"

"No, I suppose I ought," I said.

The crowds on the stairs were thinning. "C'mon," he said, "let's case the joint together."

I dipped my face into my drink. "Uh-uh, you go ahead. I'll explore later, I think."

"O.K. So explore. . . ." He set his glass down in the base of a huge philodendron plant and bounded up the stairs . . . I hoped I hadn't offended him. But I really wanted to enjoy Nikki's pictures on my own. I didn't even want Nikki looking on alongside me.

I was nudging my way through miniskirted and pants-clad gals, long-haired youths and elegantly groomed ladies in Lily Pulitzer or Pucci prints when I heard:

"Well, I guess I don't get to dine with you tonight either."

"Peter . . . how great!" I swung around, and he was standing there, his lips curled ruefully, swirling a swizzle stick around and around, pensively, in his drink.

"You know this brother of yours is a great lad, but he

is getting in my hair. He has definitely set me back months of concentrated devotion."

"Ah, Peter, you know that isn't true. I'm utterly devoted to you—in my way—but Nikki and I have so much catching up to do . . . it's been so long. Pete, look"—hoping to be conciliatory—"I really intended having dinner with you tonight. Nikki, too, so you could get to know one another better. I'd kind of planned on it, if we hadn't had to return to the villa."

"You're going back there tonight, Franca!"

"Oh, it's not my idea. It's simply that we did accept Phelps's invitation in the first place." I dropped my mouth into a kind of *moue* to suggest how unpalatable the whole thing was to me. "I simply must return for his little dinner party. It's kind of a command performance. A gathering of the clan."

"Gathering of the clan? Humph." Peter chugged his drink.

"I don't blame you for sounding supercilious. I told Nikki the whole notion of his invitation is absurd after having ignored us practically from the moment we left there. But Nikki felt we ought to go."

"O.K., O.K.," he interrupted, "don't apologize. I'm on my way." He hoisted his empty glass at me in a kind of farewell. I went and slid my arm through his.

"Ah, Peter, I *am* sorry. You do believe me don't you?"

"Certainly. But if I am being spurned in this heartless manner, I'd better get out my little black book and see who can rescue me."

"Darling," a silken voice cooed, "search no more. You are rescued." Then, "Fran, it's been ages."

"Daphne, Daphne Cotter, how too marvelous to see you. Ages is hardly the word. Let me see, it must be fourth grade."

"Mmmh, maybe for *you,* but not for me, darling!"

"Daphne, Nikki and I were at school together," I explained to Peter, remembering again how fiercely jealous I'd been of her. She was Nikki's first crush. Poor Nikki followed her around adoringly. She was in her last year at the Park School, and I think some of Nikki's earliest photos were of Daphne, her golden hair, hidden under a black wig for her part in *The Mikado*—the Park's yearly Gilbert and Sullivan performance. Daphne had had a brief career as a model, and now here she was, two husbands later, meeting us at a cocktail party on Tenth Street. Small world.

"Where do *you two* know each other from?" I asked.

"Oh, Daff's first husband—" Peter started to explain, when she interrupted with, "Father of my children, y'know," then bowed deferentially to Peter and sipped her drink, still clinging to him.

"Well, his family lived—lives, in point of fact—right close to us in Boston. We met at a cocktail party . . . where else? At the in-laws. Have to keep in touch, you know. Suppose they decided to leave the loot to someone other than the twins."

"Daphne, you are incorrigible."

"Always was, pet. But I shall take good care of Peter for you. Keep him on ice for you."

"Ah, Daffy," I said, feeling suddenly very gauche in my pants and shirt while she, in some ravishing print all whorls of silk down to the floor, but slit to her knee on one side, lolled against Peter. "But will he wish to be kept on ice?"

"Never fear. Trust old Daff for old times' sake. Come along, Peter." She kissed the air between us. "Fran, it was glorious seeing you. If I don't get to Nikki in all this crush, tell him what he knows, of course—he is a genius with that camera."

Peter blew me a kiss on the air too. I returned one on the tips of my fingers.

"Ye gods, what are we doing here, rehearsing for the Ultra Brite commercial?"

"Oh, it's you again."

"Right. And how did the exhibit go for you?" Joe leaned indolently against the wall, everything in his manner suggesting he could care less what I thought of the exhibit and wouldn't, in any case, take my observations very seriously.

"I think they're superb," I told him with what I thought to be calm, mature enthusiasm. "But then, as I explained earlier, I'm prejudiced. Nikki Grazzi is my brother."

There, I thought, that ought to hold him. I'd let him know I was not some chit of a kid who didn't know anything about art.

He lifted his glass to me without stirring from his stance against the wall and said, "I know. I'm—"

"I know, I know," I said petulantly, "you're Joe. You told me."

He shifted slightly. "Umm, what I was going to say was that I am a friend of your brother's of long standing and you, of course, are Francesca. He's told me a good deal about you."

"I'm sorry." I held out my hand, "You must think me an impossible brat. I didn't mean to be rude."

"I know. Just prejudiced." He smiled. I was right about his eyes. They were twinkling at me behind that very serious mien. "I'm not your cup of tea," he added.

"It's not that at all! It's just that—" I stopped when he laughed. "C'mon, you're mocking me."

I saw Nikki maneuvering his way toward me now, sliding between groups of people and bartenders balancing trays. He caught my eye and motioned toward the exit. I was almost relieved to be so rescued. "Look, Joe," I said, "I'm awfully sorry I have to dash at the moment. Gotta get Nikki back. But it's been great meeting you. Let's all get together as soon as we get back to town. We'll be back right after this weekend, O.K.?" I hoped I was making proper amends.

"You betcha," he said and smiled genially and clung to my hand just a little too long. "And you know I just might see you *before* this weekend is over."

Afterward, talking to Nikki, I thought about the way Joe had said that. It seemed to me, with hindsight, that it was almost the first time today he'd been serious. And his eyes hadn't been smiling at all. In fact, *I* thought on reflection, he looked quite grim. I put it out of my mind. First things first. Getting back to the villa was the most immediate thing on the agenda.

I must have dozed off once on the drive home. Probably the sudden assault of fresh air after the cigarette-laden, no-oxygen, choked rooms and the martinis. We were riding through the village, what there was of it, when I came awake. The road was wholly dark except for the half light in the drugstore and the blinking yellow caution light at the approach to the Park entrance. We swung left, off the highway, toward the Park, waited for the guard to open the huge gates to the familiar Jag, then roared our way toward the crossroad, our headlights picking up the arrow indicating West Lake Road. The light drizzle which had started just as we left the city continued to fall and the dark, warning clouds in the distance indicated that later a heavier storm was due. I was glad we were going to be back before it really came down.

"You know, Nikki, I don't think I shall ever return here no matter how often, without remembering that very first time. I can even remember what you wore."

"Good girl."

"No, truly, and Mummy, too. I can see her so slim and pretty in that ugly black—"

"Stop it, Francesca!"

I was startled by the harshness in his voice. And, when I saw that little nerve in his cheek begin to jump, I shut up quickly and sank back on the seat beside him. He seemed to relax.

"Sorry." He took one hand from the wheel and reached over, patting my knee, "But that's morbid."

"O.K. Let's talk about your show, then, Peter loved it. He was chagrined we couldn't all dine together."

"I didn't get to see him."

"I know. He left early. I think he was a little upset, actually. But I'm glad he made the show. He does know art, you know, and he thought your work was great." I was about to tell him about running into Daphne and would he believe after all these years . . . when we arrived at that sharp curve in the road and Nikki slowed.

As we swung out of the curve, a car's headlights picked us up, growing from two small spots of white light that seemed to speed toward us to massive, blinding balls of light. Nikki adjusted the rear-view mirror. "Now what the hell does he think he's proving?"

"I don't know, but I wish he'd get off our tail," I said.

Nikki slowed as the road narrowed upward, so we seemed to crawl along its edge. The driver's horn startled both of us. Nikki muttered something under his breath and slowed even more. Evidently the driver got the message, as his car dropped back a few lengths as the road began to rise against the mountainside, the earth falling down below us to the lake. Suddenly, as the road swung around a precipice of rock clutching the mountainside, the trailing car gathered momentum and, headlights flashing on and off, roared past us in a blur of white, forcing us to the edge in a screech of brakes. I clutched the edge of the bucket seat, braced myself, and waited for the impact as our car careened across the road, skidded, spun around, and almost pitched headlong into the lake. There was a scrape and crash and we shuddered to a halt.

The car was well away, its taillights pinpoints in the

dark before Nikki or I could even realize what had happened. Impossible to even image what license the car might have borne or even what make of car, the only discernible thing about it was that it was white and, judging by the fintails on the rear, of rather ancient vintage. But I was still so shaken none of that seemed to matter. All Nikki said was, "What the hell was the matter with that guy! He damn near drove us right into the lake."

CHAPTER EIGHT

I shut the bedroom door behind me and slumped against it, my breath coming in short gasps. I realized then I was still badly shaken from that drive around the lake.

As though by tacit agreement, Nikki and I had let ourselves in very quietly. We were relieved to realize that preparations for dinner must be under way as no one was in sight. Not even Boots with his suggestive leer etched across his face. Virginia and Willie, I supposed, must be changing. The house was strangely quiet. From somewhere in the other wing there was the muted sound of a stereo. Someone might have forgotten and gone off leaving it turned on low. We had climbed the broad stairs carefully, and I couldn't help noticing that Sieppi had been at his job, leaving the long table in the upper foyer banked with magnificent peonies and rhododendron leaves. The small tables at the head of the stairs held round cloisonné bowls filled with low dark greens. The house, although quiet, had an air of expectancy about it, as though a party was in planning. Apparently no matter what happened at Villa Belsola, Sieppi, like St. Francis, went about his business.

We had stopped outside Nikki's door and I'd whispered to him that I, for one, proposed to shower and change and try to recoup my equilibrium and wouldn't go down until the last possible moment, so I'd knock and let him know when I was ready. No sooner had I spoken than I had that awful sense of nagging misgiving. Did Nikki resent this continuous hanging onto him? I hoped not. And I hoped he remembered this entire visit here was his idea—not mine. I wanted out—and home. However, his response now was so negligible as to make me wonder whether he'd even heard, or taken in what I was saying. On the other hand, it could well be he was, like myself, preoccupied with the matter of that car and our near miss with the lake. I was still completely shaken by that experience, and I was sure he must be, too.

I tossed my sweater on the bed, put on the bedside light, and kicked off my clogs. But I couldn't rest. My mind was going round and round like a hamster in his cage, locked in useless motion on his wheel. I went in and turned on the bath. I considered, as I did often, that the next best thing to a hot cup of tea for soothing one's shattered nerves was a nice hot bath.

There was no way, I resolved, sloshing the delicious jasmine scent in my bath, that I could pretend some irresponsible youth, some hot-rod enthusiast had tailed us around the lake. No way! Nor could any stranger, someone unfamiliar with the Park, risk careening around that lake. No, whoever it was that tailed us had done so deliberately with the express intention of running us off the road and into the lake. But why? Until Nikki and I returned here, we hadn't an enemy. Well, we were certainly making up for it. Here at the villa, one would be hard put to recognize one's friends.

Reasonably and rationally I could not pretend, no matter how much I despised her, that Mrs. Dudley had got in a car and set out to drive us into the lake. No, I could not quite visualize her in that role, whatever else. Come to think of it, there was no one—short of Gretz, whose special province was the cars—I could imagine trailing after us. Unless someone had been hired for that express purpose. That wasn't as farfetched as it might seem. One read often of people being hired to kill . . . to kill! I caught myself. This was beginning to get more out of proportion than my hang-up about the chapel. Yet, why were these things happening. They could no longer be considered a coincidence. Oh, why had we ever come . . . and why didn't we leave? Why couldn't Nikki *understand* . . . the water in my bath gurgled and slumphed down the drain. As I rubbed myself dry, I realized I was more geared up than when I'd slid into this bath—the sole purpose of which had been to soothe and relax. Better to get ready and go down.

As I dressed, I kept my eye on the clock and realized there was still time before the dinner gong would go off. I went to the french doors and stood staring out, thinking how people isolated or trapped up here must spend a good deal of time staring out windows. I could hear our Nanny chastising us: only domestics dawdle about, staring out of windows . . . so much for Nanny. What, in any case, had I expected to see? Certainly, not what I saw: Nikki walking carefully across the lawn headed toward the lake! *Nikki* . . . I wanted to call out after him. What idiocy was this? What in the world could he be thinking of? I pressed my face hard against the triangle of glass in the doors as though I might will him to look up, will him to return to the villa. Then, close behind him was Uncle Willie. No mistake, that was Uncle Willie. I could make out the forms in the lights from our main gate. For a moment I thought Willie was trying to catch up with Nikki, join him. But as I watched, every now and then Willie would drop back a pace, slow down, and I realized that Willie was not trying to catch up with Nikki but he very clearly did not want Nikki to know he was behind him. He was, in fact, stalking Nikki, always at a respectable distance. I wanted to fling open the terrace doors and call out a warning. But what warning? What did I actually know? What was I afraid of? What could Willie possibly do—or wish to do—to Nikki? And I realized I was not that concerned about Willie. What really concerned me was Nikki. I could worry about Willie later, if at all. What mattered now, the only thing that mattered, was Nikki. Why was he out there? And why headed for the lake?

It was no use. No matter what agony went on inside me, the plain fact remained that there was Nikki, Willie following, headed for the lake. I watched as they both disappeared from view.

I could barely concentrate on getting ready, but about twenty minutes later, dressed and coiffed, a dab of Chamade behind each ear, I was on my way down to dinner.

I felt like some character in a novel. I came down the wide stairs, one hand on the rail, the other holding my long skirt so I would not trip and break my neck, thus putting a perfect end to this bizarre weekend. Dinner, I knew, must be ready. However, one would never know, as such plebeian scents of cookery did not permeate the house. They were, one assumed, wafted out the service entrance by some super-electric device or buried under some delicate, aromatic household humidifier. The two huge candelabras—they must be six feet tall—twelve candles in each—were already lighted in the dining salon while soft dinner music came from the small sitting room where, to my surprise, Phelps, Virginia, and Willie were already waiting.

"Ah, my dear," the voice of Phelps Warton, our stepfather, took me by surprise. "Welcome, welcome. It was good of you to come," he said in a voice quivering with emotion. He greeted me with outstretched arms, pushed along in his chair by Boots, with Dudley at his side. "Good of you to come," he repeated in a sort of breathless monotone.

I went toward him. He was not at all as I remembered him. Or was it that time had left its mark on him and not the others? He was wearing a navy blazer, an ascot at the neck of his open-throated shirt, ensconced in a wheel chair, his shoulders massive. I remembered, then, for no reason, he'd been captain of Harvard's football team. What trivia runs through one's mind at such moments! His face was round and puffed like boiled rice, maybe from drinking, although I had no recollection of his drinking to excess. And, maybe it was the unhealthy pink-and-white plumpness suggesting that close to he might smell of some extravagant men's cologne that gave him a sickly aura. His eyes were small in his round face and a faded blue. I could see the pale pink of his scalp through the silken glistening of his white hair. He took my hands in both of his, blue-veined now with age, and pressed them together gently.

"Francesca, my dear. A beautiful woman. And why not?"

He made a deft gesture with his wheel chair and said: "Come along, Boots, move about a bit. Dudley, see what you can do for our guests, perhaps some Coulommiers cheese that Mrs. Trent enjoys and a few biscuits, please. Whatever Mrs. Dudley feels would not spoil the bounteous repast she has prepared for us—ah, Nikki"—he dismissed Dudley with his hand—"there you are."

I took a deep gulp of my drink, determined not to make any special observation about Nikki's appearance. He looked well groomed and quite rested. He had decided, I gathered, to defer to our host and was wearing a navy blazer, gray knit bells, and Guccis. Nikki, I thought, you're an actor. We were together. Whatever else, his strange meanderings hadn't done him any real harm. And harm to Nikki was the thought uppermost in my mind.

Dudley had moved off stiffly on Phelps's command, and as the door of the pantry swung wide I saw, from the edge of my eyes, that Mrs. Dudley had the tray already prepared and was holding it aloft for Dudley. With a quick jerk of her head, she indicated he was to take it straight back, be quick about it, and get back in there. In the few moments it took to observe this little pantomime and under general cover of conversation, almost all of it directed toward Nikki and the show and how it had gone, Phelps leaned forward to me and said:

"Francesca, please come to my study tonight after the

others have retired." His eyes shifted uneasily with a kind of frenzied urgency. "You *must* come. It is imperative I talk with you before any more time—" I saw the look in his eyes, the lids lowered once, quickly. I straightened.

"Oh, fine," I swung round, "do you trust me to make it, Phelps, or would you rather Dudley make it—oh, here he is now." I looked over my shoulder toward Phelps, as though confirming a conversation about preparing him a brandy. "Would you rather, Dudley, if you're not too busy? I'd hate ruining Phelps's good Courvoisier . . ." I hoped I'd carried it off. I moved into the room with the rest of the household.

We made a perfect drawing-room tableau. Virginia was spreading a water biscuit with her favorite cheese. "I didn't mean to usurp the role of hostess . . . it's simply they've laden me down with all these goodies."

"Aunt Virginia, I adore being waited on and I know Nikki does. Mmmh"—I bit into a cracker—"delicious." I scooped the crumbs from the edge of my mouth delicately and said, in as casual a voice as I could manage, "By the way, Nikki, did you catch a nap at all?"

"Nap!" Phelps sounded as though any young man caught taking a nap must be out of his mind. I caught myself, thinking, why that particular cliché . . . out-of-his-mind. An ordinary, commonplace phrase which suddenly took on sinister connotations. No. He sounded as though he felt any young man who took a nap at this house couldn't be quite normal . . . And there it was again, all those phrases beginning to raise their heads with ugly implications. Well, then, let's just say Phelps felt, if actually he did have any feelings, *disapproving* of any young man who found it desirable to nap on a fine evening . . . and let it go at that.

"We had a horrendous drive," I tried to explain to him. "We were nearly driven into the lake by some clown. I think that on top of the excitement of the show left me —for one—quite depleted."

I could feel Virginia and Willie looking at me patiently, tolerantly. Why did I always feel I had to explain? Shut up, Francesca, I charged myself.

"You were saying," Uncle Willie prodded.

"She was asking," Nikki said.

"Ah yes, you were asking if Nikki had managed a nap. Did you Nikki?" Uncle Willie asked.

"Well, if by nap you mean sleeping—no, but I must confess I lay down, stretched out on the bed and—"

"And you might have dozed off," Virginia offered, patting her still perfect coiffure in place.

"I don't know what this great conspiracy is to put me into a nap before dinner," Nikki said, "but I suppose it is possible I might have dozed. Why"—he looked from one to the other—"is that bad, or something?"

"Darling, don't be silly. I was only making conversation. I was simply exhausted myself. But how did we get into this verbal hassle?"

"Well, did *you* nap, Francesca? Now that you brought up the conversation to nap or not to nap."

"What an inane conversation." Phelps swung his chair around. "Shall we go to dinner?"

"Let's, by all means . . . and let's drop it. No, I did not nap, Uncle Willie," I told him, "did you?"

"Well, like Nikki"—Uncle Willie held out my chair for me while Nikki waited on Aunt Virginia to be seated—"I couldn't swear to it. I was puttering around my room, but this kind of weather does make one drowsy."

"What you're saying is, then, Uncle Willie, like Nikki you may not have slept but you didn't leave your room."

"Ye gods, shades of Hawkshaw the detective," Phelps laughed.

"How very odd you sound, Francesca," Virginia said.

"Well, I guess I am odd. I did not nap. I didn't rest. I showered and wrapped myself in my old terry robe and then went and stood looking out the window. You know," I explained, feeling all the while how rotten I was being, "those lovely french doors, what a terrible temptation to fling them open and walk out onto the terrace and simply soak up all that glorious country air . . . well, there I stood and I could have sworn"—I stopped and popped a baked clam in my mouth hoping I'd caught my audience's attention—"I could have sworn, up until this conversation, that I saw . . . first Nikki, collar upturned . . . I mean," I said, being properly facetious, "who would be out *without* their collar upturned in this weather . . . stomping along toward the lake." I waited. No one volunteered a word. I went on, "And behind him . . . guess who?" I hoped I was making some kind of impression on someone.

Dudley poured wine. Mrs. Dudley cleared the first course. "Behind him," I said, pausing for effect, "bringing up the rear, I could have sworn was Uncle Willie."

Silence.

"You're sure, darling," Virginia suggested, "you weren't sleeping, dreaming, maybe?"

I was tired of this. I was tired of Phelps acting as though he were a spectator at the Meadow Club tennis matches, popping his head from one to the other. Why didn't he say something? Do something? I stared straight at Willie now and asked: "Uncle Willie, were you outside walking in the rain? Whether you were following Nikki or not is wholly immaterial."

"I feel, Francesca, as though we were winding up some kind of soap opera. You can't be serious, Fran," he said. "I assure you I do not meander about in the rain, much less would I be following your brother, which, after all, appears your chief concern."

"And obviously, Fran, he could not have been following me," Nikki added, "as I was in my room."

"Oh, I give up!"

Phelps smiled. "Well, fine, I wondered if our entire meal was to be devoted to who napped and if so when and where."

I lifted my glass to him. "Phelps, do forgive me. I think I've been frightfully rude, a bore, and really quite stupid."

"I'll drink to that." Nikki laughed.

Everyone laughed then, and the atmosphere became more relaxed. That is, relaxed for everyone but me. I knew I could not possibly challenge Nikki now. Or Uncle Willie either. But the fact remained they were lying. Both of them.

CHAPTER NINE

I was so upset by Willie's evasiveness if not downright lies I almost forgot Phelps's urgent message for me to meet with him in his study when all the others had gone to bed.

I moved around my room restlessly. There were so many unanswered questions whirling around in my head I began to feel I'd never find the time or climate in which to sort out all this confusion.

Why had Willie and Nikki both lied? They were almost strangers. Nikki hadn't seen Willie since his return until this weekend. Maybe—I began to try and sort pieces—maybe Nikki hadn't intended to lie to *me* at all. Maybe *I'd* been precipitous. Maybe Nikki hadn't wanted Willie to know he'd been out there walking around the property and maybe, until I'd mentioned it Nikki hadn't even realized Willie had been out there, too. I preferred to think it was something like this, something Nikki would explain to me when we were alone. All I had to do then was wait.

I got out of my long skirt and sweater top and pulled on the old jeans and body shirt. If I was to meet Phelps and wait until the others had retired, it was certainly not an occasion that called for the formality of an evening skirt!

From the french doors, even without stepping onto the terrace, I could see through the shimmer of rain onto night-dark lawns illuminated by lights from our gatehouse. And directly beneath my window, squares of orange light flattened on the lawn, reflections from the windows lit downstairs, were suddenly quenched out. The household was preparing to retire. While I waited until it was the appropriate time to meet with Phelps, I would be able to hear Nikki when he returned to his room. And, I was sure, if my conjecture was correct, and he'd only wished to deceive Willie as to his whereabouts, he would stop by my room and explain everything before he went to bed. He wouldn't want me to worry.

By the time all the familiar footfalls had faded, doors closed discreetly, lights doused one by one through the house, I had to conclude that, whatever Nikki's reasons, he had no intention of sharing them with me this night.

I waited another five or ten minutes until I was sure the villa was packed in for the night, then I put out my bedside light, drew the curtains across the doors, because although I was not going to be in the room to look out onto the dark wet night, I felt more secure, more comfortable, enclosed in the room, as though in some way I was shielded, protected from whatever dire elements walked outside the villa.

I stepped cautiously into the dimly lit corridor and followed the twisted reds and blues of the hallway runner toward Phelps's study—maybe partly from memory, as making my way along this corridor was like returning to my childhood. The ancient floor sighed with each step I took, so I had to stop and nervously listen for some response. Silence. A long, dark silence that stretched its way like a giant abyss down the length of the hall. I would have been more comfortable if Nikki had been with me. And in a way that puzzled me. It was Nikki who'd jumped at the chance to return here. Why wasn't he included in this meeting? Why had Phelps so obviously excluded him? Nikki was right; I was beginning to read sinister implications in the simplest of acts.

The corridor broke off to the right as it neared the stairs and as I turned, feeling my way along the wall, I could see a faint blade of light cutting under the study door. I tiptoed to the door, oblivious as possible to the squeaking boards, as though my ignoring the noise would prevent others from hearing it. Standing outside, lifting my hand to knock, I had the overwhelming sense of something sinister permeating everything and everyone in this house. I took a deep breath and knocked, gently at first.

No response. I knocked a little harder, then froze, the sound of my knock echoing like noise in an empty barrel.

I waited a long moment, pressed tightly against the door until I could feel the stillness settling around me again. I tried the handle and the door gave easily, swinging into the gloom of Phelps's study.

The lamp was lit on his desk but the rest of the room was in complete darkness. I had some difficulty adjusting my eyes to the sudden glare of the lamp, and when Phelps wheeled his chair out of the shadows of the corner of his study, I saw he was ready to retire. The blazer had given way to a robe and a pale green pajama collar was opened out over the neck of his robe. Without the ascot I could see how scrawny and aged his throat was under the round, puffy face.

"Come." He held out his right hand to me, patting the edge of the studio couch with his other hand and said, "Come sit alongside me. I want—I must—be quick about this, child." His voice had dropped to an almost inaudible whisper and there was a kind of agitation about him, different from the agitation he'd shown before which made me suddenly sorry for him. It was as though having carefully thought out his plans, his decisions made, now confronted with the actuality of the scene he was not quite able to act. He seemed immobilized, disintegrating before my eyes. He was rambling now and his speech came in short breaths. "My dear, it is difficult for me to explain . . . be patient with me. There are going to be very many changes. You must be prepared. Complete changes in your life . . . Nikki's . . . all will be as it should have been—" He put his hand to his forehead in a gesture of almost utter confusion. He seemed to realize much of what he was saying made no sense to me. "I understand after all this time. But, Francesca, all will be well. It will be resolved. Trust me. Do you understand? No, how could you. Listen. . . ." His lips were dry, his tongue sticking to the roof of his mouth as he tried to articulate. He moistened his lips with the tip of his tongue. Suddenly he appeared to gain control of himself. He reached out and grabbed my arm. "I want to now. But I cannot, I cannot."

"Cannot what?" I asked gently. I could not understand at all what he was struggling to say, but I hoped to alleviate this dreadful sense of anxiety and frustration. He leaned his head back against the chair, exhausted by this interior struggle. "I cannot explain . . . very hard for me . . . cannot explain. But I will, I will. I promise. Before it is too late." He was becoming so agitated again, it frightened me. "In the meantime my dear, please listen. . . ."

I was listening. But he didn't seem to comprehend this. I was listening although I did not know for what.

"Be careful. Do you understand . . . no harm must come to you. There is danger. You must be careful." He pressed my hand gently, and I held his hand between both of mine. He seemed, at that moment, like a confused child.

"Phelps, please don't be worried. Everything will be fine. You ought to rest now. You can explain everything, anything, that is troubling you, later."

His eyes were closed. I wondered had he even heard me. He opened them slowly now and sighed. "You're probably right," he said.

I did not feel in the least that he believed I was right, but maybe it was the easiest way. "Good night, Phelps," I said. "Try to rest."

He lifted his head, straining toward me. "Francesca," his voice was hoarse, pleading. I turned to him. "Be careful. Please . . ." I nodded. His head sank back against his chest and he rolled his chair away, turning his back to me. I left the room, closing the door very gently behind me and collided, outside, with Dudley!

"Aah, you startled me." I backed away from him.

"I'm sorry. I was looking for you, Miss Franca."

"Oh . . . ?" I knew I sounded unnatural as though I didn't in the least believe he had been looking for me. He dug his thumb and index finger into his waistcoat pocket and drew out a folded slip of paper.

"I must apologize, miss, but Mrs. Dudley took this telephone message whilst we were serving coffee. I fear she forgot to deliver it. I trust it is not important."

"Thank you," I said, and pocketed the note without even glancing at it. "Good night, Dudley." He stepped back to let me pass.

I walked back quickly to my room, feeling his eyes piercing the back of my head. He made no motion to retire until I'd reached my door. Then he stalked back along the corridor to the servants' wing, leaving me alone and relieved to finally close myself in my room.

I unfolded the note. It was a message from Peter to say he was staying with the Cotters. He and Daphne were at the club and would hang around until about midnight if I could get back to them.

It was much too late to ring them now. I'd call them in the morning and ask them to lunch. After all, if we were to be trapped here we might as well make the best of it and we could do with a bit of cheer. Daphne was always gay and fun and at this moment, Peter appeared a solid rock from my old life to which I wanted to return as quickly as possible. This house could use a little cheer.

Even through the drawn curtains I could see, as I got into my night things, the flashes of lightning singeing the night. It sounded as though it were going to storm all night—what was left of the night.

Despite the noise, I dozed off. It must have been the storm that wakened me. My bedside clock said two-thirty. I lay quiet, listening. Above the sound of the pelting rain and the recurrent rumbles through the mountains of thunder and the searing flashes of summer lightning, there was a persistent clicking sound and the shudder of the doors. The wind . . . ? No. Someone was trying to get into this room from the terrace through the french doors! My first reaction was sheer, unadulterated rage. How dare they-him-her-it-whoever attempt to break into my room! Then, as I came more fully awake, I remembered Phelps's warning: *Danger . . . Everywhere . . . Be Careful . . .* I lay perfectly still, breathing evenly, pretending to be asleep. If it were not for the occasional shudder of the doors, the clicking sound might easily be mistaken for some small rodent gnawing in the walls of this old house. But I knew better. I got up and, armed with nothing more threatening than a flashlight, crossed the room stealthily and flung back the curtains. Just at that moment a sheet of lightning tore across the sky. I reacted automatically and shut my eyes. When I opened them, there was nothing but torrents of rain pouring down in a constant stream and sporadic sheets of lightning illuminating the sky and then, in a burst of light, there was Nikki! He was walking across toward the gatehouse again, head bent against the buffeting wind. There was no mistaking that old corduroy jacket, collar upturned, and shielding his face, pulled down, the old canvas hat he sometimes wore in inclement weather. I stepped back abruptly, half hidden behind the drapes. I had the unhappy feeling *should* he look up, *should* he see me there at the window, he might think I was spying on him. In a way I was doing just that. Although, actually, if someone, some strange noise, hadn't wakened me, I should probably have slept straight through the storm.

By now, Nikki had disappeared from my line of vision. This meant if he were headed in the direction of the chapel he would have to cut back into my view again. If he didn't appear again, that could only mean he was returning to the villa and his nocturnal prowl, for whatever reason, was completed. So if he didn't reappear I would know he was returning to his room. I waited . . . currents of chill air whirled around my bare feet. I felt chilled, like ice, and I was trembling. I waited but he did not reappear. I dragged the curtain back across the window and shut out the night and the storm.

To challenge Nikki now might prove dangerous—dangerous for him. I was beginning to feel more strongly than ever now that this return to the villa had been a great mistake. I began to feel as I had earlier in Nikki's illness when they explained to me about his medication. It was essential for him to be on medication which would affect his behavior, the doctors explained, yet at the same time the doctors warned if there was any marked change in his behavior or what they referred to as character or personality changes, I was to alert them. And I remember how I'd reacted to this worrying, watching, looking for signs that might or might not be interpreted as personality changes. How could I, a lay person, really know what was out of character for Nikki after that long siege of illness. What was the drug and what was *normal* . . . I was beginning to have the same frightening feelings. I didn't want to react like this but I could not help feeling the villa was having a very detrimental effect on Nikki. If this were not so, then how explain this behavior?

I waited to be sure Nikki had returned to his room, knowing, sooner or later, he must be confronted with this behavior. And if, as I felt, this environment might be threatening to him, then, certainly I had to think of some pretext, something to get him away from here before anything more permanently damaging happened to either of us.

The house was settling down now with those obscure night sounds these ancient houses make, battered by the elements. I threw my robe over my shoulders, put my feet into the old terry scuffs and let myself out as silently as possible and down the hall to Nikki's room. I tapped at the door very gently. No response. I had no notion of what I should have done had he answered, but figured, in my desperation, I would worry about that when I came to it. I turned the handle very gently, leaned against the heavy door, and let myself in.

A small night light burned in the far corner of the room. Nikki lay in his bed curled on his side, sound asleep! Or if he were not asleep, certainly feigned it. Oh, Lord, what a nightmare of suspicions our life had become. But it seemed amazing to me he could have fallen into such a deep sleep so quickly. In the dim glimmer of the night light I could make out the shape of his jacket hung over a chair alongside his bed. I did not have to put my hand to it to know it was saturated. He must have been prowling around in that rain for hours to become that soaked. His canvas paddy hat was stained black with rain and was tossed on his bureau, while his boots, wet and muddy, were set just inside the bathroom door. On the night table were the rows of accumulated pills. Perhaps this might account for his going off into this sound sleep so quickly after returning to his room. But reasons no longer mattered. Nikki might have the best possible reasons in the world for why he'd been out there in the night, but I was convinced now I must get him home. Whatever it was that haunted and eluded him, what locked secrets he hoped to unlock here—could not, must not—be further pursued here. If there was any real danger, as Phelps had implied, the danger could only be to poor Nikki. Somehow I had to get him away from here and back to the city.

CHAPTER TEN

When I'd finally got back to my room and into my bed, my mind was churning with the night's events. Nikki lying there sleeping so soundly when only moments before he had been trudging around in that pouring rain didn't make sense . . . what was Nikki thinking about . . . what was going on in his head . . . I was frightened . . . frightened for Nikki. I thought I would never get to sleep and when I did it was an uneasy sleep.

I was always on the edge of a cloudy consciousness until I became aware of sunlight coming into the room. Sunlight! I took that as a sign . . . "the year's at the spring, the lark's on the wing . . . God's in his heaven" . . . I think . . . even though everything is not "all's right with the world."

I lay there for a moment luxuriating, stretching, then turned on my side, propped on my elbow and thought how I could, if I wished, have a tray in bed. Well, now that would be novel. However, my New England puritanism came to the fore. That was a soft way of living . . . one ought not even attend such an idea . . . up, up, shower and dress, I commanded myself.

I stood looking out the window. How different everything appeared, how sane, in this morning light. The rain had stopped finally sometime during the night and now the greenery in the garden was sodden. I pushed open the doors, the air was deliciously fresh and touched with that after-rain smell of damp earth. I saw Sieppi coming along the road. Darling Sieppi. There he was with that same crazy outfit of Mexican straw hat, regardless of season, the World War I jacket and baggy trousers that ended in Newmarket boots. He'd make a great hippie. I watched as he came along with great masses of flowers carried in an old wicker basket. He was going toward the rear of the house and presently disappeared from sight. I slipped into the old jeans and shirt, shoved my feet into the clogs—this whole ensemble was fast becoming my uniform—and went down to try for a cup of tea.

Downstairs in the kitchen, Mrs. Dudley was arranging flowers.

"Good morning, Mrs. Dudley. Aren't they lovely!"

She stopped, put down her gardening shears, wiped her hands along her apron, and without turning went to the stove. "Tea, isn't it?"

"Oh yes, thank you. But please don't let me interrupt. I can wait until you're finished." I waved my hand vaguely in the direction of the flowers laid out neatly on a damp, day-old newspaper. The kitchen shone starkly white and antiseptic in the bright sunshine.

"No trouble. The kettle is always on."

"I'll be glad to fix it myself and then you can go on with your floral arrangements, if you wish. Oh, how sweet . . ." I leaned over from my perch on the high kitchen stool to admire a single bud in a crystal vase surrounded by sprays of baby's breath. "How lovely. Is it for Mr. Warton's tray?"

"No," she said, and moved it away abruptly.

"Well, all the arrangements are lovely. The peonies . . . mimosa . . . just everything," I said self-consciously.

"Mr. Warton likes flowers all through the house, all year round. He leaves the choice up to Sieppi whatever he fancies to grow in the nursery."

This appeared to bring our conversation to an end. I sat in silence drinking my tea, after assuring Mrs. Dudley I did not care for anything to eat with it. Tea finished, I excused myself to go upstairs and change. No comment. Mrs. Dudley went on with her cutting and snipping.

Why did it seem so necessary for me to explain everything to this miserable woman as though I had some neurotic compulsion to win her approval? An approval she obviously withheld from me and Nikki—and indeed had withheld from our mother as well. But Aunt Virginia. Ah, that was different. I heard the echoes again of our mother's voice . . . *"You never liked me . . . it was always your little Ginny."* Well, probably our mother had been right. But this didn't matter now. Our mother was gone, nothing could change that. As for Mrs. Dudley, I was probably reverting to the childhood pattern. Immediately we set foot in her domain, I remember how as children we always felt she never liked us and that probably the reason was she'd felt with children in the house there would be more work for her. But now there was no need to pretend any longer. The fact was simply that she did not, had never, liked us.

Marching along, back to Nikki's room, I could feel myself becoming enraged just at the very thought of that woman.

"Nikki . . . are you up?" I tapped apprehensively on the door.

"I will refrain," he said, opening the door to me bare-topped, clutching his pajama bottoms close to him, "from the observation about catching the worm. I take it it *is* morning?" He sounded himself as though last night had not really happened.

"That it is and I've just been down and had a dish of tea with the loquacious Mrs. Dudley." I nudged myself into the room.

"Make yourself at home, sweetie. You don't mind if I shower and shave, do you?" Nikki asked through the closed door of the bathroom. "Have you something special on the agenda that you come calling at this hapless hour?"

I looked around the room. There was a half-finished breakfast tray. I told myself I was sleuthing. One had to begin somewhere. I noticed his jacket was gone, too, and his hat.

"Nothing in particular," I said.

"What . . . ?" he yelled over the water.

I went closer, mouthing the words at the door. "Can you hear me?" He shut off the water. "What . . . ?"

"I said—"

"Don't shout," he said coming to the door now, rubbing his hair briskly.

"Sorry." I flopped down on the unmade bed. "I said I had a call from Peter—he stayed over at Daphne's. I thought we might ask them for lunch . . . something . . .

this place is really getting to me. What are you wearing?" I said, pretending to help choose a tie.

"No matter."

"Where's your jacket?"

"Guess Dudley took it. Y'know the old valet bit. Bet if I put my shoes outside the door last night, they'd have been shined, too. D'ya ever get the feeling you could learn to like this kind of life . . . valet service, breakfast in bed, all that jazz." He waved his hand, holding the comb, to encompass the room. "Guess I'm to the manner born." Then he stopped and looking at me through the mirror, swung around, and, leaning against the bureau said, "You aren't listening, Franca. Franca, what's the matter?"

"Nikki, you know I didn't want to come here, right?"

He nodded agreement. "You know," I went on, struggling to find the right words, the appropriate words. "I came because you seemed to think we ought. It was important, for some reason to you." He was certainly listening, being attentive to me. "Well, I don't really know what it is that's so important to you here . . . but Nikki, I want to go home."

He laughed, almost with a kind of relief, I thought. Or did I imagine this, too? "Franca, darling, we *are* going home. Is that all that's troubling you? After all, we've only been invited for the weekend. We can't—as much as I might kid about the soft life—really stay on, like the Man Who Came to Dinner." He was crouching now to get a full view in the mirror as he combed his hair carefully. "We have to leave tomorrow in any case."

"I want to leave right now. Right away, Nikki. I hate it here. I mean it. I really do." I felt near to tears.

"I know. But we can't leave now." He wasn't smiling. He was deadly serious.

"*Why* can't we?" There, it was said. It was out. Direct. Answer me, I thought.

"I can't tell you. At least not right at this moment."

"Like"—I held my breath and took the plunge—"like for instance you can't tell me what you were doing wandering around in the pouring rain at night?"

"Fran, we aren't going into that did he or didn't he nap routine again, are we . . ."

"No." I swung myself off the bed and moved toward the door. "I mean last night."

"Last night . . . I don't understand. What do you mean, *last night?*" There was a slightly mocking tone as though he were mimicking me when he said "last night."

"You weren't outdoors last night in the teeming rain after everyone else had gone to bed? When I, for example, went off for my interview with Phelps?"

Nikki came and put his arm around me, holding me off so he could look straight into my eyes. "Francesca, I do not know what you are talking about. I was not anywhere last night except dining with you and then to bed"—and his tone was lighter now—"what's this about your meeting secretly with Phelps? Aha, *you* didn't report that to *me.*"

"Nikki, please, be serious for a moment. You honestly say you were not out on the grounds last night . . . wearing the corduroy jacket, the old paddy fishing hat, and.

. . ." my voice trailed off. He was looking straight at me, his eyes wide with wonder. He was telling me the truth. That is, the truth as he knew it. For if Nikki had been out there last night, he did not remember.

CHAPTER ELEVEN

The meeting with Nikki so upset me that all I could think about was getting him away from here. This was not the place for Nikki. No matter what he thought. I was sure he was retrogressing. The episode of the night prowl of which he had no memory was typical. I was in an absolute panic. Suppose he should retrogress to the point where he could not be retrieved? I began to feel frantic . . . worse, helpless. There was no one to whom I could turn—no one who understood Nikki's problem except, of course, the doctors, and I knew, inexpert as I was, that to introduce the notion of doctors at this point was unthinkable. I was even frightened of what the thought might do to him! But something had to be done, and quite obviously I was the one who must do it. But what . . . ?

As I'd left Nikki's room and started back down the hall, Mrs. Dudley was making her mid-morning rounds to see if beds had been made, rooms vacuumed, fresh flowers, all plans for the day ahead, and I thought, as I did often, how the unimportant, simple little acts of the day help us to keep our sanity. The day went along—beds did get made, meals were planned. One went to work if one had work to do. No matter what agony and screaming went on inside one, these things got done, mercifully, they had to be done. She had stopped me in the hall and asked how many there would be for lunch and to tell me Mr. Warton would not be joining us. He was not feeling well. I might have reacted to this differently if it were not for Nikki's problems, his well-being which took precedence over everything else. I made some noncommittal comment and said I hoped he'd feel better as the day progressed and before I could tell her how many for lunch, she told me she'd heard a car pulling up just as she'd left the kitchen and wondered did I expect guests. I didn't, I told her, but would go down at once and see who'd arrived.

Outside in the sunshine the world looked less grim, and seated on the terrace, enjoying the sunshine, were Peter and Daphne.

"Sorry we didn't ring you first," Daphne apologized, waving her sunglasses at me, her sun-tanned legs stretched out in front of her. "Peter wanted to phone. He's very proper, your young man, I must say."

"I'm so glad you've come, you wouldn't believe. No need to call. You'll stay for lunch, of course." Anything, I thought, anything that would get us through this day.

"Well, I must confess that was our intention. Unless you and Nikki wanted to join us for lunch at the club, but it's awfully dreary, I think it only fair to warn you."

"No, this is absolutely great. Nikki will be down shortly. We all slept late this morning. Phelps is incommunicado, but Aunt Virginia, do you remember her at all, Daff?—well, she's here and Uncle Willie, too. I must tell Mrs. Dudley we'll be six for lunch."

The words were only out of my mouth when we heard

a car making its way up the hill and waited while it turned in and headed along the yew-lined drive toward the villa.

"I think," Daphne said, putting her hand to her forehead like an Indian scout, "you'd better set another place, luv."

The car pulled up to the terrace and leaning out of the driver's seat, Joe said, "Do I park here?"

I felt a sudden surge of joy, and my pulse skipped, gone as quickly as it came under a wave of embarrassment. How could I possibly feel such elation for a guy who yesterday I hadn't even known existed?

"Anywhere you like. But if you're staying awhile, pull up around the rear gate . . . who knows"—I knew I sounded almost giddy—"there may yet be other guests."

He swung the little two-seater around and tore off. In a matter of minutes he was back and looking more like Nikki than ever. Did they, I wondered, have some secret signals! He, too, had shed the blue jeans in favor of a more conservative pair of slacks, topped with a Lacoste shirt. He seemed much taller than I remembered, but then anyone is taller than I.

"Well, this is a surprise. A very nice one. Nikki will be delighted," then because of the rather wry smile he shot at me, I added, "and I'm delighted, too, of course."

As if on cue, Nikki appeared. "Well, looks like a little farewell luncheon."

"Farewell? Why? Is somebody going somewhere?" Daphne asked.

"Home eventually," I interjected. "After all, this lush

life can't go on forever. I'm a working woman, y'know—which reminds me I'd better get to work and warn Mrs. Dudley about our luncheon guests." I was glad to get away for a moment. All you have to do, Fran, I kept telling myself, is to get both of you—you and Nikki—through this day. And I realized then that I'd not only been pleased to see Joe but relieved. Hadn't he said himself he and Nikki were old friends of long standing? It must be true, too, or he'd never drive up here uninvited and unannounced. They must be close friends. How silly I had been. Things were definitely looking up now.

Mrs. Dudley was not, as I'd anticipated, in the kitchen, and I could not finds Boots or Dudley, either. I started back upstairs, thinking she might still be making mid-morning rounds or even tending Phelps if he was really not feeling well. And, while I was up there, I'd look in on Virginia and tell her we had guests for lunch. Maybe the whole day might be brighter for us all.

Virginia's door was ajar. She was leaning over her suitcase, rummaging through it. I tapped lightly on the opened door, leaning my head around the door jamb. "Aunt Virginia, just wanted to tell you we've got a veritable luncheon party going on downstairs. I've been looking for Mrs. Dudley to alert her and also wanted you and Uncle Willie to know."

She swung around. "Oh, yes. Yes, thank you." Her face was flushed and her mouth trembled when she spoke. She looked as though she had been crying.

"Aunt Virginia," I came full into the room now, "are you all right? Can I get you something?"

"No, no I'm fine, thank you. Well, perhaps a glass of water . . . ?" Her face suddenly appeared ashen to me, and I remembered that coughing spell last night and wondered, if maybe, there was something really wrong with her and she wasn't saying.

"Of course, darling. Stay right there and I'll bring it to you."

I glanced around the room once, quickly, and saw Mrs. Dudley had forgotten the water carafe, unless it had been left in the bathroom. I went in to look for it and at the sink almost knocked over a tiny floral arrangement that Virginia or someone had placed in the basin to get water. It was the same floral arrangement Mrs. Dudley had been working on this morning in the kitchen. As I waited for the water to run cold for her drink, I moved the little crystal vase around and around, it was so charming and delicate . . . then I saw the card . . . it had been crumpled as though someone had crushed it out of all recognition. I smoothed it out. It was a quite ordinary, inexpensive, linenlike card, the sort sold in small packets in stationery stores. Written in small neat letters, typical of British County Council school penmanship, the card read:

"Welcome home, my Virginia. Love, Nanny."

Nanny? Obviously Mrs. Dudley had put the flowers here and just as obviously this was her handwriting, her card. But Nanny . . . ? Mrs. Dudley? She had been with them long enough . . . she *could* have been their Nanny. That thought had never occurred to me. *Had* she been with them that long? But wouldn't Mummy have mentioned this . . . or was that what our mother intended to imply when she'd said Dudley had always favored "little Ginny." *Was* that what our mother had meant? Was that why Mrs. Dudley hated us so . . . because she felt Virginia ought to have had the house? Welcome home . . . the card had said. Was that the implication intended? This would explain why she hated Nikki and me so much, too. I could visualize an old couple like the Dudleys, childless, becoming involved with a family, devoting their lives, developing a kind of proprietary concern for the children and Virginia, obviously their favorite . . . funny though, that Mummy never mentioned she'd been their Nanny. Well, no matter. I intended to put the whole crazy pattern of this life out of my mind—for the present.

I took the water back to Virginia who half sat, half lay along the bed. She had chewed most of her lipstick off and seemed suddenly to have aged right before my eyes. This house was surely not conducive to any kind of joy or relaxation. I tried putting on a cheerful air.

"Please do feel better, Aunt Virginia. We have guests for lunch. Quite unexpected but I think it might be fun—a little change. A friend of Nikki's whom I only met yesterday at the show, and then there's Daphne Cotter—well, she was Winston—she's Winston Cotter now. Do you remember her at all? She remembers you—Aunt Virginia, what's the matter?" She had put down the glass in a hand that was trembling and I saw the way her face was working she was trying to hold back tears.

"Nothing, dear. Truly, nothing at all . . . I'm just awfully tired, I think. Perhaps I ought not to have come. The trip up, the excitement." Her voice trailed off. "If you don't mind, I think I won't join you and your nice young friends for lunch."

"Of course. I understand. Do rest. Shall I send Uncle Willie up to you?"

"No! Well, I mean," her voice dropped, softened a little, "well, I really don't want to worry your uncle. I think maybe he'd enjoy the guests."

"Right. I'll go tell him and Dudley, too. I'd certainly better tell her or we won't have any lunch. Now rest, dear. Promise."

"I promise," she said, so wearily I felt we should all be much better off when we got away from here.

On the way downstairs my spirits lifted a little. I was sorry about Virginia, of course, but was consoled with that misery-loves-company bit. For if Aunt Virginia was so adversely affected by the villa, it meant it wasn't just *me*.

Before going downstairs I decided to peek in on Phelps. Last night and our entire conversation now seemed a kind of nightmare—something I might have dreamed. I wish I had dreamed it. I wish I'd dreamed seeing Nikki wandering around out in that rainy night. I wish it had all been a dream and would disappear, vanish, crumble into dust in the bright sunlight of this day. I got as far as the entrance to our wing when I saw Mrs. Dudley coming out of Phelps's room.

"Oh, Mrs. Dudley, how is Mr. Warton?"

"He's not feeling well at all, miss. I've just taken him a cup of soup and he'd like to rest." She did not say in so many words I was not welcome to visit him, but I very definitely got that message. I decided I should not press it for now and I did have to let her know about the guests we were having for lunch. I felt apologetic.

"I hope it isn't putting too much work on you, Mrs. Dudley. It was all quite unexpected."

"No problem at all, Miss Francesca. We are always prepared for extra guests. Is there something special you'd fancy or will you leave it to me?"

"I'd be grateful for your help. Your menus are always delicious." Well, that was something I could say in honesty, however grudgingly.

"Very good then. I'll send Boots out with the drinks."

I watched her move down the hallway to the stairs. Hesitating before Phelps's door, I debated going in, as Mrs. Dudley was rather unsubtly suggesting I leave him alone. I couldn't suppress the discomfort last night's conversation had caused and was sure just one moment with him could do no harm. I didn't knock, afraid if he were resting I would disturb him, but rather eased the door open. He was lying on his bed, bathrobe closed tight at the throat, eyes shut, and a strange, chalk-white pallor aging his face even more than years had done. He was asleep. I could hear the struggled efforts for breath as his lungs seemed to battle with the thick warmth of the room's air. The half-finished cup of soup sat on his night stand, the rim of the cup caked with cream-colored substance. I lifted the cup to my nose and smelled. Bitter. I put it down. Whatever it was, it didn't smell too appetizing. Leaning toward Phelps, I could see a thin line of the creamed film over his lips and a narrow trickle that had run from the corner of his mouth and dried like a piece of cracked skin.

Leaning over like that I neither heard the door open nor saw Mrs. Dudley until she called.

"You are neglecting your friends," she said sternly, her eyes straightening me up. I felt suddenly weak-kneed, the child caught in the cookie jar with no ready excuse.

"I was just. . . ." I started weakly.

"Snooping, pestering, bothering. . . ." For the first time I sensed her losing the icy grasp on her emotions. The cold hostility sounded more like hatred.

"I was concerned," I apologized, feeling myself weaken in front of her strength . . . resenting it . . . but afraid of it.

"If you were really concerned you would leave. You and your brother. You may never know the depth of the pain he has caused here." The icy control had returned.

"What do you mean?" I could hear my voice betray me. The calm strength I wanted to convey dissipated in the whine of my words.

"We are disturbing Mr. Phelps." She motioned me from the room, following me out and shutting the door. "If you are as concerned as you pretend, you'll leave and take him with you." Her voice was scathing.

"Him . . . ?"

"The brother. Your brother. You've both brought enough trouble and sorrow to this house. Let the old man die in peace. You've no call to torture him like this—go."

"Mrs. Dudley"—I struggled to control the quivering rage in my voice—"I think you are overstepping your role. Not to mention the bounds of good taste. May I remind you we came at our stepfather's invitation. You can be sure *we'd* never wish to return here. If there is sorrow in this house, we've had our share of it. It is not a place I should choose to be, so I feel your attitude is quite out of line. You might like to consider at the very least an explanation—if not an apology."

"Explanation, is it? Ha . . ."

I could have smacked her.

"Let me tell you, you'll rue the day you pushed me into this. Explanation you want, is it? Very good then. Here it is for what it's worth. It's your brother Nikki. He killed your mother and it's Mr. Warton himself witnessed it. What a burden to carry and he's carried it all these years. Wonder it didn't kill him long since, carrying that knowledge locked up inside him all these years—just to protect the boy—and all for the love of your mother. Now he cannot carry it any longer. He must clear everything. The strain has become more than he can bear and the presence of that Nikki here"—she made his name seem like an obscene epithet—"has nearly done him in. Why do you think Mr. Warton asked you here?" She didn't wait for my answer. "To clear it all. He's lived with this knowledge of your brother's crime all these years and couldn't carry it to his grave with him. Now after he's called you both here, he doesn't feel he has it in his heart . . . the conflict's all been too much for him. Should he throw it all up to your faces, or let it rest? It's all been too much."

I stood in shocked silence while she continued her monologue.

"It was Ian, Mr. Dudley, found the boy—he saw the whole thing himself as well. Driven blind with rage, he was, that boy, with your mother's drink and his own jealousy of your stepfather, robbing you both of the proper joy of your childhood, ruining your lives. Ian didn't find him trapped above the rocks. He saw him struggle with your mother in the boat and she, too drunk to fight, too tired of life, I think. Ian dragged him up from shore and protected him as he would his own son. Small wonder he was in shock with no memory. Or so he *said. My* poor husband, it's cruel, that's what it is, to give a body such a burden. Ian had always been close to the boy. You'll recall that yourself . . ." Her voice seemed to change now as though another, a different mood had taken hold of her, wheedling now. "He was always looking out for the boy, helping him with his camera, setting up the trips for his animal pictures . . . like his own son you might say. And all these years trying to protect him."

I remembered, reluctantly I had to admit, I remembered Ian had always been kind. Especially to Nikki.

"Look, girl, you must go. Go quickly. If all this comes out—if he insists on rehashing all this," jerking her head in the direction of Phelps's door, never taking her eyes from my face, "we'll all go down in ruin. Go—and take that sick murderer with you."

CHAPTER TWELVE

She may have said something else to me before she went, leaving me to sink against the hall wall with the sense of watching my own death, but if she had I didn't hear. I groped. Frantically . . . desperately . . . the way I imagined someone might when they are losing their sanity and are vaguely conscious of it—conscious enough to search for some order as though to find that order, no matter how contrived, would mean there was some hope.

I searched for that order, leaning there against that wall, emptiness spreading out at broad angles beside me. And I cried. A silent, convulsed cry that swelled and enveloped. I felt no anger. No real fear. A void. Just an all-encompassing void.

"Oh, God, oh God, oh God . . ." mutterings I wasn't even conscious of until I heard them—my voice but yet not my voice. A voice vague and forlorn.

She could be lying. I wanted her to be lying. How could she hate so much to lie like that! I'd rather it be hate than truth. And if she couldn't hate that much . . . if it were true . . . then what? Was Nikki any less my brother? Did I love him any less? I couldn't. No. *No no no no* . . . I couldn't. It only meant that Nikki was . . . had been . . . more disturbed than we'd thought. That perhaps, after all, it was best he did not remember . . . that the true horror of our mother's death should never be remembered. Was that best . . . was it—I couldn't—I didn't—know.

I stood bracing myself against the wall, breathing slowly, deliberately, as though physical control would lead to emotional control. I moved down the hall toward my room, tasting the salt of tears on the edge of my lips. I could not let one hateful woman control my thinking. It still might be a lie. And yet looking back . . . Nikki's severe reaction, sending him off so quickly, all the vague unanswered questions . . . it seemed. . . . No, I was doubting too soon.

In the room I fell on the bed, shutting my eyes to the blank exposure of ceiling. I was falling into Mrs. Dudley's hands. Regardless of whether it was the truth or not I was playing her game. I could never let Nikki or anyone know this . . . not now . . . not yet. For now I must be the perfect actress and with this resolved I sprang from my bed.

Washing my face, I decided to bury my feelings as best I could . . . for as long as I could. I would dress in something suitably sporty and carry it off like a thirties' movie heroine.

I washed, changed, brushed out my swinger hairdo, and with one quickly muttered prayer went down to join them on the terrace.

True to her word, Mrs. Dudley had sent Boots out with the drinks. He shoved the portable bar onto the terrace and was taking everyone's order.

"Fran, I wonder someone here in the Park hasn't tried to steal Dudley from this household long ago. He is a jewel. He even remembered I drink martinis. Thank you, Dudley," Daphne said as she took the glass from him.

"And thank you, madame."

"There," she lifted a golden eyebrow at me, "see what I mean. He's simply too perfect."

Dudley went on mixing drinks and Boots arrived with a huge floral centerpiece for the lunch table.

"Mrs. Dudley asks will you be lunching out here on the terrace, Miss Francesca?"

"I should think so, Nikki, right? It's so heavenly out here." I was very conscious of my tone, trying to keep it light.

"Oh, is Mrs. Dudley still with you as well?" Daphne asked.

"Naturally," Nikki volunteered. "Could you imagine them ever being separated? They sort of go together like the proverbial Gold Dust twins."

"Yaah, well, they were once."

"Were what?" Peter asked. "I'm not at all sure I am able to follow this conversation."

"I was just saying," Daphne explained, "that the Dudleys were once separated."

"Come, come, you don't mean legally," Peter making a joke of it.

"Course not. But you remember, Fran. Or maybe you wouldn't. It would be your Aunt Virginia who'd remember . . . the fall she went back to Boston."

Peter lifted his glass in a mock toast. "I knew Boston was bound to get into this somewhere. I'll drink to that."

"No, I don't remember that at all, Daff. I think probably we hadn't come back here yet." I feigned interest.

"Well, I only remember because Virginia, your aunt and my older sister were best friends."

"That's right, I remember hearing somehow, somewhere. . . ."

"Ah," Daphne interrupted, "God knows what you might have heard about those two."

"Family gossip. Great. I'm all for it."

"Nikki, you liar. You know that's not true."

"I know, Franca, but it sounded like something I ought to say. Anyway, Aunt Virginia can fill us in herself when she comes down."

"She's not coming down."

"Foiled!" Nikki turned back to the bar.

"She's really not feeling well," I added.

"I don't like to suggest, since I'm only a kind of uninvited guest, but the climate can't be too good here. Mr. Warton not well. Mrs. Trent not well. My, my . . ."

"I think," I suggested, "lunch is ready. Shall we take our drinks to the table?" I didn't want to think about my stepfather, nor did I want to think of the misery on Virginia's face. I only knew I had to hang on through this day . . . and then we'd be off and away.

Boots served under Dudley's watchful eye. Mrs. Dudley did not put in an appearance but this was understandable as she'd had to plan and execute this luncheon on very short notice and had done, as usual, admirably.

"I shall have to play at least six sets of tennis to work off this marvelous lunch. Do I hear anyone for tennis?" Most of the table groaned. "Well," Daphne insisted, "we're going to have to work this off somehow."

"Trust you, Daff, you'll think of something."

"Aah, there's Mrs. Dudley," Daphne got up to greet her. "Do you remember me at all, Mrs. Dudley? Daphne Cotter. I was Winston and my sister Consuelo Winston was Virginia Bascome's best friend—Fran's Aunt Virginia. They came out together, in fact," Daphne was addressing all of us, "at the Autumn Ball here. . . ." Then she frowned and hesitated for a moment. "No. No-o. Now I remember . . . see," she turned in mock triumph to Nikki. "Knew I'd remember. No that was it . . . she *didn't* 'come out,' she became ill. Virginia, I mean. And had to go away and that was when Mrs. Dudley went—"

"Excuse me, miss. I have work to do." Mrs. Dudley picked up the coffee tray and, terminating the conversation, marched off to the kitchen.

"Well, really now . . ."

"Obviously, *Mrs.* Dudley could take a few pointers from *Mr.* Dudley," Peter suggested.

"I'm sorry, Daphne. She was really quite rude."

"The penalty of being our friends, I should think, alas," Nikki said.

Daphne with her dogged persistency and her taste for gossip continued. "I was only trying to prove my point. I was right. I did remember. It was when your aunt was so ill. She had to go to Boston to see some bigwig specialist and Dudley went along with her—I was only a child myself but I remember all the hassle about who'd go with her because Consuelo, of course, wanted to go—after all, Virginia was her best friend. But the family vetoed that. Connie simply had to 'come out.' No way! And the tears and the commotion. How could one forget. So finally it was agreed that Dudley would go with her and while Dudley was there in Boston, she looked up a family she'd once worked for."

"That's very interesting. When had she worked for this family? I mean when she'd first come to the States, or more recently?" Jumping into this little bit of gossip seemed a welcome relief.

"Careful," Nikki warned me. "You're falling right into Daphne's gossip trap."

"Uh-uh. Just interested."

"Well, I'm not the absolute authority, but I take it she'd worked for them just before she came to your family . . . like maybe two years previous."

Well, then, obviously she hadn't been their Nanny. I don't know why this seemed so important to me. But there was just something about that that nagged me. Everything about that woman, let's face it, nagged me.

Daphne had finished with her saga now. How Dudley had gone up to Boston with Virginia and then, finally, decided she wouldn't go back to her former employers after all.

"So then she came back to us and lived happily ever after, right?" Nikki looked around to us all for confirmation.

"Well, that's one way of ending it," I said. "Come on, this is silly and it's getting boring."

"Do you mean to say you find my saga of the Bascome girls boring? I'm hurt."

"Here, have another martini," Peter said, "and you'll feel better about it."

I was thinking only another hour or two hours have passed but maybe with a little luck the others would pass like this, too, and soon we'd be putting this place behind us forever. I looked up to find Joe staring at me. He looked away abruptly when he saw I'd caught him. I thought again: whatever else, he is here . . . if I can only get him alone . . . talk to him . . . I know he could help.

At that moment, as though he could read my mind, he said, "What about a drive, Fran? Daphne and Peter seem set on a game. There's nothing much to interest us at the club. How about showing me the countryside?"

"That's a great idea, will you come along, too, Nikki?"

Nikki declined but insisted I go. I felt torn. Should I or shouldn't I? And where, it just suddenly occurred to me, was Uncle Willie? Did he and Nikki have some rendezvous planned?

"O.K. I'll run up and change into slacks, something more suitable for country hiking. I won't be too long."

Halfway along the corridor to my room I heard voices coming from Phelps's room. They were loud and they were angry. The voices were Phelps's and Mrs. Dudley's.

"No one intends to wait. You get that straight. There isn't time. They've got to go. And I mean now."

"There won't be any time for anything if this isn't taken care of first." That was Phelps's voice and it was feeble. "What must be done, must be done."

"I'll agree there, but our meaning is different. They have got to go. Both of them. Nikki and her . . . I warn you if not, there'll be trouble. Bad trouble. You'll see. And you'll have that on your head as well. . . ."

"Stop. *Stop it,* do you hear!" I could imagine poor Phelps clutching his head, his hands over his ears to shut out the sound of this monstrous woman's voice. I was frightened. I stood rooted to the spot although I realized any minute the door might fly open and she'd come storming out. Instead I felt a warm breath close to me, and there was Dudley himself, almost on top of me!

"Was there," he asked with a false kind of deference, "something you wanted, miss?"

"No. Well, as a matter of fact I came to get a scarf, Mr. White is taking me for a drive, and I heard—er— voices . . ." Dudley stood there, implacable, immovable, saying nothing while I stammered on. "I hope Mr. Warton is all right."

"I'm sure he is, miss. Do you wish me to deliver a message?"

"Thank you, no," I said moving quickly toward my room. "I'll see him when I return if—that is—if he's feeling up to it."

I had all I could do not to race down the hall and lock myself inside my room. I was grateful I was going to be able, finally, to share all this with someone who would understand.

I rushed into my room, picked up the nearest scarf at hand and started right back down the stairs. I could not wait until I was downstairs, the terrace in sight, to go out and join Joe.

CHAPTER THIRTEEN

I tried not to appear as though I were racing back down the corridor. I moved with just the proper degree of haste appropriate to a young female going to meet her date, but inwardly I was screaming and racing. I knew Dudley had moved along to the rear stairs with his usual elegant, silent tread; nevertheless, all the way down the broad stairs and out the door I felt that some magic eye, which I was not convinced he must possess, was following me all the way. At the terrace I stood still and, pretending a nonchalance I did not feel, carefully whipped the kerchief over my head, tucked the spears of hair behind my ears and looping the ends of the kerchief around my neck, tied it in a loose knot at the nape. Then I hoisted the strap of my bag a little as I saw Joe sitting patiently in his two-seater. He'd been drumming his fingers against the wheel and looking toward the terrace with a quiet, smiling, anticipatory expression. When he saw me he made a motion as though he was going to get out and come round to open the door for me. But as I stood fastening the kerchief his smile seemed to fade and in a timesaving gesture he leaned across the wheel, swung open the door and reaching out for my hand, almost dragged me into the car. I knew then that the sickening fear I felt at my encounter with the Dudleys must show in my face.

Once we'd left the yew-lined drive and the gardens and trees and the villa itself had disappeared from view, the little car picked up speed and raced along West Lake Road, moving quickly in the direction of the gates and the exit from the Park. After the heavy rains the delicate needles of pine, drenched with rain, were now soaking up the sun, and the air was redolent with their scent and all the damp fresh earth smells. If, I thought, one could give oneself up to all this magnificent light, air, sun, and green, how could there be a care in the world. Also, I could not pretend that driving along with Joe seated beside me did not give me an enormous sense of security. I glanced at him now surreptitiously. I could not tell if he knew I was looking at him because of the dark sunglasses he wore—rather like those worn on the ski slopes. He seemed to stare straight ahead and I thought again how like Nikki he was in his style. His lip curled upward in a barely perceptible smile. He knew I was staring at him! I averted my eyes, quickly.

"Now," he said, "this is your territory, Francesca, whither away?"

We were at the gatehouse and I realized how for a few brief moments I hadn't thought about the villa, my fears, nothing. Wa-it a minute . . . I admonished myself.

We were outside the gates now. To the left was the side of St. Mary's Church facing onto the little cemetery enclosed inside its own fieldstone wall, and away, as far as the eye could see, Route 17 ran through the Ramapos and beyond to Monroe and finally cut its way through the upper regions of Orange County. To the right were scattered buildings that composed the village and the Roman Catholic church our mother teasingly liked to remind us was "off limits." The Park was largely Protestant, and tradition had it that the very first owner of the villa—that family for whom it had been built—had "gone over to Rome" and with that passion and zeal of the convert had been instrumental in having the church built. She deplored the fact that for years there had been no facilities for Roman Catholics—most of whom were largely domestics working in the Park "mansions"—to practice their faith. Certainly they had all been welcome to attend Mass in the chapel when the family were in residence, but that was mostly only in the spring or summer, hardly a solution for those faithful who required a permanent place to pursue the faith. I used to wonder sometimes if perhaps the chapel had a curse put upon it because our family had let it fall into disuse. I shuddered as I did always when I allowed myself to think of that chapel.

"Well," Joe prodded, "where to?"

"Let's see. I think the direction we take will depend on your interests. Are you, mayhap, historically orientated?"

"That I am . . . a born historian!"

"Good. Turn left then and head toward Sterling Forest."

"Sterling Forest . . . ? I thought," he said as the car roared away, "that was a day-outing kind of thing. Y'know . . . the Gardens and all that jazz. . . ."

"Come, come now. Who's conducting this tour and who ever said we were going to visit the Gardens?"

He made a mock gesture of beating his breast.

"O.K. then," I said in a firm voice, "turn left again at the first intersection."

We did.

The countryside in all its lush greenery slid by, now and then its beauty broken, for me, by ugly houses, clapboard, of no particular architectural persuasion with a new garage or maybe a car port stuck on like an afterthought. Glass jalousies at doors and windows and ceramic deer or dwarfs dotted their lawns. I was delighted when we'd driven deeper into the forest and saw only paper signs tacked on trees indicating all this land was posted. We continued to drive deeper into the woods. We did not speak. But I had that peaceful sensation that we were in some strange way communicating with one another as indeed we were with the nature all around us.

We came into a clearing. "Now," I told him, "just here . . . if you pull just over there." I pointed to the tall brick chimney, "I shall give you my super-special guided tour. Come to think of it," I said as he came around this time and helped me out of the car, "it's not so much a guiding as a lecturing. This is it."

"Which is . . . ?"

"Oh, yes." I pulled off my scarf and looped it through the handle of my bag, ran my fingers through my hair and said, as we made our way over pebbles and stony mounds: "This is one of the early furnaces of Sterling . . . just visualize, if you can, long-haired youths, like yourself, some of them wearing perukes and bows and buckled shoes, all working frantically to forge those chains that were to protect the Hudson and West Point from the British invaders. In those days, these hills belonged to the Lenape Indians. Mahwah, New Jersey—now a Short Line bus stop—was translated as 'the meeting place' and Hessian soldiers defecting from the army fled to these hills and married Indian maidens and black concubines who had been 'imported'—legend has it—for the pleasure of British troops. Their descendants still live here and there is the romantic list of names, Dutch and Hessians, you meet everywhere . . ."

"Francesca, you are a veritable fountain of information."

I glanced at him from the edges of my eyes. I could sense the nervous energy in my delivery as though spewing out some concrete facts dispelled the nebulous anxiety I felt about Nikki.

"I wasn't being flip," he said, "I find it fascinating. These trees . . . for instance . . . once upon a Boy Scout time . . . I seem to remember we learned how to determine the age of these old landmarks . . . but in lieu of that, just think whatever their actual age they were here all through that period, they breathed that same air as those now long-dead patriots. It is, as you said, almost incredible that this little sample of that life remains intact." He reached out his hand to me. I took it.

"And if you'd like a touch of the European, I might add that most of the various workers in these mines in the early eighteen hundreds were Polish or Italian immigrants . . . matter of fact, the signs warning of the dangers of some of the materials and so on, were posted in Italian. We *do* get around, don't we?"

He pulled my arm through his now, hugging me closer. "Thank God. Yep, you certainly do."

"End of lecture."

"I'm disappointed. And if I'd known this magnificent wilderness lay so close at hand I should have suggested a picnic lunch. We'll do it another time. Can we make that a project? Once you're back in town, we'll make a special excursion up here complete with champagne."

"And watercress sandwiches. Do you like watercress sandwiches? They're rather dainty for a man but they're *delicious.*"

"Watercress sandwiches it is. I'll bring the watercress. You bring the champagne, O.K.?"

"Joe, you're a nut. . . ." We stood together for a moment, not saying anything. As though this spot had a special enchantment—just for us. But as we scuffed our way back to the car I knew, the moment we were headed back to the villa, I was also headed back to trouble. And that was really one of the true reasons I'd wanted this time with Joe.

He held the door for me, pulled my scarf free of my bag and tied it around my head babushka style. Then he bent over and put his lips, lightly, on the tip of my nose. "There, that's for now . . . and where to now?"

I reached out my hand touching his sleeve lightly.

"Joe . . . I need your help . . . I don't quite know how to say this . . . maybe it's because I realize you and Nikki are close friends that I feel free enough to talk to you." I could hardly look at him. I kept my eyes staring down into my lap as I went on talking. He reached out and folded both of my hands in his. "Talk. . . ." he said.

"Oh, Joe . . ." And in that moment I knew I was so frightened I couldn't talk to him in the firm, rational way I'd hoped and everything just came pouring out.

I told him about the scene in the corridor, the conversation I'd overheard, and then finding Dudley spying on me.

"I know it sounds paranoid, my using the word spy, but quite honestly I truly feel that was exactly what he was doing."

Then I explained, too, about the conversation with Phelps. I knew my voice sounded taut and strained and I kept thinking: Be calm. He'll only think of you as a hysterical woman. I could have wept with relief then when he swung around, took off his sunglasses and said, "Relax, Francesca. Unwind for a moment. And if it will help, let me tell you I don't think you're paranoid. I very definitely feel you are right. There is something wrong in this house—ha," he gave what is often referred to in fiction as "a hollow laugh" and added, "that's got to be the all-time understatement."

"Oh, Joe, I'm so glad. Glad, I mean, you don't think I've flipped." Then I went on to tell him about Virginia and Willie and the whole weird atmosphere but making a concerted effort not to mention Mrs. Dudley's accusation. That was something I had to wrestle with by myself. Something I might never mention to anyone, even Nikki. "I don't understand anything—and I'm worried about Nikki. Joe, listen, you've known him for so long. I mean you know he's been ill. Well, I mean. . . ."

"Yes," he said very quietly, "I know something of Nikki's illness. We never really discussed it."

"Oh. . . ." I don't know exactly what that meant. I could hear the sound of my own voice straggling off on that *Oh* . . . It could mean almost anything.

"But see, Joe, that makes it so much easier. For me, I

mean. The fact you can *really* understand my fears for Nikki."

"Fears . . . ?"

Did I imagine it or was Joe suddenly withdrawing from me, withdrawing his support from me, moving away, lowering some kind of curtain between us.

"Yes. I don't think this was wise for him. You know—thank God you *do* know and can help—what a nightmare this place has been to Nikki. Everything—" I could feel myself filling up. I should despise myself if I cried. Oh, God, no. "Everything that happened to him happened here at the villa. It was he who insisted we return. It was crazy. We should have never returned here, Joe. I'm afraid for what's happening to him."

"What's happening? You haven't told me anything. Just how fearful you are." He slid his sunglasses back on his nose with the top of his index finger and stared straight ahead.

I hadn't imagined it. He was annoyed with me because of what I was saying about Nikki and far from understanding what could—what I believed was indeed happening to Nikki—he felt for and with Nikki. They were together. I was outside. Now I really could have wept. I felt I was utterly alone now and somehow I had to help Nikki.

"Joe" I reached out again, touching his arm tentatively—"Joe . . . you think I'm foolish worrying about Nikki."

"I don't think you're foolish, Franca, not at all. It's just that you can't seem to realize Nikki is well now. He's O.K. Don't worry about him. You gotta let go—as they say—he's quite able to do his own thing and do it well."

"O.K. When he wanders out in the rain, then denies it? Or worse, has no memory of it? When he wanders off for hours in the hills, around the lake as though it held some macabre fascination for him . . . that place where he almost had a relapse?"

I knew there was no use in pursuing this any further. I didn't know what or how much he and Nikki had discussed. Perhaps I was hitting him with too much and if he really didn't know the extent of Nikki's illness, then I would sound like a neurotically possessive sister. I hoped my own attitude toward Joe, my response to his attitude, didn't suggest I felt differently toward him, that I was now behaving like that bratty sister he'd first met. Felt differently? How did I feel toward him? I hardly needed to echo that question. It was abundantly clear that I hadn't ever felt this way toward anyone. I recognized this must be the way Peter felt about me! And although I knew I'd never ever really entertained serious thoughts about Peter, I'd never felt anything but an affectionate friendship for him . . . and I also realized I had never before ever been in love!

The rest of the ride was made almost in silence. A silence quite different from the earlier one. I was angry with myself. Angry at feeling as I did . . . that I'd messed everything up.

Back at the villa he helped me out, then turned studying the now threatening sky, went to the trunk, opened it and pulled out a coat.

"I've enjoyed every minute." He was leaving, then. "And I enjoyed the guided lecture tour." He slid into the front seat and smiled. The whole world suddenly came back into focus. He put out his hand and held onto mine. "And, Franca, if you need me, call." I nodded dumbly. "I'm serious," he said. He jerked his head in the direction of the villa. "This is a weirdo of a place, y'know. I'll be happy when you're back in town."

Then abruptly he shifted gears, the motor roared and over the sound of the engine he said once again: "Call. Don't forget. O.K.?"

It was then, just as the car pulled away down the yew-lined drive, that I noticed the coat. It was the same bright red plaid I'd seen from my window the first night at the villa.

CHAPTER FOURTEEN

My immediate reaction to seeing that coat was precisely the sort Joe and Nikki would chastise me for. There must be thousands of raincoats in that popular glen plaid, and how could I be sure from my bedroom, peering through the tiny glass pane into the night, that it was the same? Obviously I couldn't. Besides why on earth would Joe be slinking around in the rain with Dudley. And yet . . .

I watched his car until it swung around a curve and disappeared into an arch of trees. Although our meeting hadn't gone as I'd hoped I nevertheless hated to see him go. I felt a strange kind of loneliness. I couldn't help thinking how negative his response had been to any suggestion about my fears for Nikki. Admittedly I'd only intimated at Nikki's strange behavior because of Joe's lack of response. Now I felt that his warmth and strength, his presence here, had made me feel all at once as though I *were* imagining things, that I was just letting this place get to me. He hadn't even shown a glimmer of concern about what I'd said or my fears for Nikki. But now, left alone here, I desperately wished he were back with me and I wished I'd been stubborn and obstinate and insisted on telling him *everything*. As I turned back reluctantly toward the house it seemed to loom up ominously in all its massiveness and I felt again that almost sick tremor of anxiety that I'd felt on the very first moment of my arrival. I couldn't resist the urge to turn back once again in the direction the car had taken, hoping I would see Joe racing back up the driveway with some forgotten message . . . something . . . any pretense that might bring him back. But Mrs. Dudley, standing dourly in the doorway, brought me back to the somber reality of Villa Belsola.

"The luncheon went very well, Mrs. Dudley. I do want to thank you." I refused to admit how much she'd disturbed me.

She mumbled some response far more honest than mine —it was blatantly hostile.

"Has my brother returned yet?" I asked her retreating figure.

"I have no idea," she said indifferently. She certainly did have an idea. She knew. She knew if anyone took a deep breath in this house, so it was absurd for her to pretend she didn't know.

Standing in the hollow shafts of sunlight flooding the living room, through the glass doors of the patio, I couldn't help frustrating myself with mock assassinations of Mrs. Dudley.

Why couldn't I follow Nikki's advice and ignore her rather than succumb to her perverse pleasure of annoying me? At least Sieppi, whom I could see hunched over a batch of zinnias, seemed pleasantly receptive to my company. I opened the door and stepped out onto the flagstone terrace. I hated to disturb Sieppi; he seemed so furiously intent as though his gnarled hands drew energy from the vibrant colors surrounding him. My shadow arrived first, falling in front of him so he turned before I spoke.

"Come to see how my garden grow?" he asked.

At least he smiles, I thought. "I can see how it grows—beautifully."

"I like to hear that, say more."

We laughed.

"Sieppi, have you seen Nikki?" I asked. The smile left his eyes but he tried to hold it on his lips.

"He was here. He was walking around." Sieppi waved in the general direction of the lake.

"How long ago?"

"Not long. Maybe half hour." He paused. "It's no good. It's no good."

"I know," I said softly. "Thank you." He didn't answer. He had turned back to the soil.

Walking toward the lake, balancing myself against the sloping lawn, I had the feeling of eyes, staring down on me like fingers on the back of my neck. When I turned Sieppi was gone, but standing at the glass doors, drapes shrouding her, was Mrs. Dudley. I couldn't see her eyes but I could feel them—invisible glass tubes stretched across the lawn to probe me. The drapes moved and I was alone.

The lawn grew steeper nearing the water, just an elbow extension breaking off from the main body to rest against a rind of shore. There was a narrow trail curving lazily like a mottled snake to the boathouse and beyond that, nothing. There had once been paths superimposed on the weeds and bushes by Nikki and me, which had led around the lake. We could follow them to the main body of water and to the cove where we would stand tossing rocks into the water, watching the rings race each other to the rising cliff. On this cliff Nikki had set up his camera and from there it was believed he had stood helplessly watching his mother drown. Until now that is what I had believed. The truth—it was all painfully locked inside him.

I was afraid he was there now, forcing himself to remember something that was probably best left buried under the years. He wasn't along the shore line, unless he had forced his way through the woods to the main body of the lake. The heavy night's rain had beaten down most of the underbrush near the boathouse, making it impossible to tell if anyone had walked through. Reluctantly I stepped up to the woods, the soft earth giving way under me, the branches snapping at my legs. Twenty yards up the woods began, its massive gnarled roots lying under the earth, forcing me to hopscotch my way through. The shadow of a path began to lift above the water and, without having reached the bend to the lake body, I was already winded. I stopped, the woods' damp odor clinging to my nostrils. Below me, on the opposite side of the lake, I could see a figure. It looked like Nikki moving slowly out of the woods to the far side of the boathouse. I waved frantically, hoping Nikki would be able to see me through the thick rectangular pattern of branches. He seemed fixed in place like a piece of statuary decorating the lawn. I hurried back down coming out of the woods about the boathouse, calling him, arms waving frantically. My words seemed to float over the water and die. He turned away. I raced to catch him, dreading the thought of going back to that house alone. Something under me—a rock or the rain-softened earth—gave way and I was struggling futilely for balance, sprawling forward, arms breaking my fall into the bushes and weeds bordering the path.

I'd seen something like this in a Marx Brothers' movie, I thought, but the vague pain in my right ankle didn't make it quite so funny. My hands were smeared with mud almost covering the tiny beads of blood forming on the surface of my palms. They stung.

"Nikki," I cried, pulling myself up, more frustrated than hurt. But he was gone, leaving me to hobble awkwardly back to the house. I was acting foolish anyway, coming down to the lake. Nikki would only laugh at me for worrying about him, or be annoyed that I had nominated myself his baby-sitter. I could never explain my feelings: my nebulous fear that being here jeopardized the years of progress he'd struggled for.

Coming over the rise in the lawn, I was surprised to see him, not entering the house but walking slowly toward the garden side. I resisted the urge to call him, standing to watch instead. It was suddenly very chilly, an ominous cloud floating over the sun soaking up its warmth like a gray sponge. The pain in my ankle told me I should be soaking it instead of spying on my brother, but I couldn't dispel the feeling that, as Sicppi had said, it was no good—that I should and must know what drew him out here oblivious to everything else. Perhaps it was unfair to Nikki making hypocritical all the things I'd said about how well he seemed, how his entire attitude and manner had so wondrously changed since the tragic years following our mother's death.

Still I couldn't help it. This aimless wandering was like picking at a wound just healed; opening hurts and troubles neither of us might be able to cope with. And if what Mrs. Dudley had said were true, if indeed Nikki were responsible for Mother's death then . . . but I did not want to come to grips with that yet.

I followed Nikki along the slate path leading to the side of the house and down to the garden, weakened now by the bite of the fall on one side and the ominous tangled greenery surrounding the chapel on the other. He was standing by the chapel door, shoulders bent under some invisible weight, arms slack at his side, looking like a scarecrow skewered grotesquely at the end of a stake.

I debated calling him but he decided for me, disappearing into the overgrown tangled weeds either into the chapel or around it. I followed, half of me wanting to rest my aching leg and half of me wanting to know where Nikki was going and why, and all of me wanting to avoid the chapel. Why is it, we outgrow so many of our childhood fantasies and fears, yet always cling to one, which lets us know we're really not so grown up after all? Well, I resented it! I hated to think I would approach that chapel with the same terror it held for me in childhood. Yet nearing it, feeling the perspiration form along the edge of my palms, I knew I was fooling myself—and not doing a very good job of it.

Hedges rose up alongside of me, a tightly knit, impenetrable wall of green-black leaves. I froze at the full view of the chapel by the entrance, head tilted in the direction of some sound like the snapping or rustling of branches.

This is silly, I told myself, hesitating here because I was

scared years ago. And with this new resolve I moved toward the chapel door. I kept my hand on the hedges as I walked, like a child running a stick along an iron railing, the substance of the branches giving me a little sense of security. Why would Nikki be there? Why did he wander like this? I felt somehow as though it wasn't fair to me. "Nikki. . . ." I called. "Nikki." Only my voice drifted to the steel gray sky.

The tangled ropes of ivy roots crisscrossed against the wooden chapel door. Something scurried across my foot. I gasped, shut my eyes tight, and stood rooted to the spot for a moment, my heart racing as I prepared for that whirring rush of feather wings, the rush that had returned to haunt me so many nights. Nothing. Only the familiar cooing of the mourning doves. There was a sudden abrupt sound, something, someone . . . moving inside . . . I forced myself forward. I pushed against the door, shuddering inwardly and it swung back with its familiar creaking sound. The dank earth smells rose up assaulting my nose. I swallowed and gritted my teeth. Fear rose like the taste of bile in my stomach and throat. I strained to adjust my eyes to the darkness after the bright outdoors. My breath and my heartbeats echoed through my skull, beating into me a fear over which I had no control. Don't, I told myself, don't panic . . .

"Nikki. . . ." It was a scream before it was a thought. Hold on, please, hold on, I told myself. My panic forming itself into a scream, clutched at my throat. I steadied myself to try and keep standing as everything blurred before me. I started to turn—an arm roped itself around my neck, jerking me violently off the ground. I twisted reaching back, my hands clawing at flesh . . . my own screams ringing in my ears. Then falling . . . falling . . .

There was light again and thin rain.

"Francesca, Francesca," Nikki's voice. Vague. Distant. "Francesca." He was drawing me up. My eyes wouldn't open. I buried my head in his chest.

"Nikki. Oh, Nikki."

"Easy . . . easy. I heard you scream but I couldn't find you. What are you doing in here?" he asked, lifting me gently to my feet.

"Ouch!" I had almost forgotten the pain in my ankle.

"What happened?" he asked. I was leaning against him, almost being dragged up from the chapel door. We were outside.

"I don't know. I was looking for you . . . someone grabbed me and . . ." I could hear I wasn't making sense but still I couldn't form the right sentences. And there were things I *couldn't* tell him. *Why* I was out there . . . why I was following him.

"Oh, Nikki," I sagged against him. "It was *awful*. I tried to fight. I know I clawed whoever it was. Then . . . I must have passed out. I don't know how long I was 'out.'"

We were at the house now, Nikki holding me up with one arm sliding open the glass doors with the other.

"Here." Nikki eased me into a chair. "Rest here and I'll get a blanket and some hot coffee for you." He was smiling at me. It made me feel warm and safe. It wasn't until he turned to leave that I noticed them. Two long scratches—the blood not yet dry—scarring the side of his cheek.

CHAPTER FIFTEEN

I slept late the next morning but felt I had not slept at all. All night strange figures, characters from the "Twilight Zone" or horror movies, paraded in and out of my dreams. I raced across endless lawns in pursuit of Nikki, never gaining on him. Or I battered and hammered away at the chapel door around whose dome bats and birds of prey whirled about in ever narrowing circles. I woke up screaming. Then, sitting bolt upright in bed, my heart hammering, my sheer gown clinging to my damp skin, the palms of my hands dripping, I realized the screams were only in my mind and in my dreams. It was almost dawn before I fell back to sleep—a sleep of utter exhaustion. I kept turning over and over in my mind that rescue in the chapel. Nikki—my attacker and rescuer? Certainly, whoever my attacker was, he must have been lying in wait for me. This would explain why there had been no fanfare of birds. They had already been frightened off when the attacker entered the chapel. So either I had been expected . . . or had surprised the attacker? Was it all planned? Or was it an accident because of my stumbling into something? And all the while I tried to put these pieces together in my mind, using the terminology "attacker"—person or persons unknown—was of course skirting the thought it could be

Nikki. Why would Nikki attack me? If it was Nikki who had been in the chapel . . . and if it was Nikki, perhaps it was not *I* he intended to attack. Maybe he'd expected someone else. Maybe I'd surprised him and he'd panicked. But if that were so—who would Nikki be waiting for? *Why* would he be waiting. And whatever the answer to attack someone, whoever it might be, was not the answer to *anything*. Nikki was gentle. He had always been gentle. Until Mrs. Dudley's accusation I'd never thought of him any other way. I did not even want to entertain the thought that something might have happened to him here because of his exposure to this tragic house once again. Maybe it was already too late and the damage had been done. Yet Joe had insisted Nikki knew what he was doing. But what did he know? How could I trust his judgment? More than that, he'd probably *think* as Nikki did and that wasn't how *I* would be thinking. The thoughts raced through my mind until, finally, I'd dozed off.

I wakened to the sound of someone running the vacuum along the upstairs corridor. It was eleven-thirty. I supposed if I rang I could get a cup of tea. But the thought that Mrs. Dudley might be the one to bring it up dissipated that idea at once. I simply could not face her now. I had to think.

I pulled on my old blue jeans and as I dressed thought how much I wished I could see Nikki and find out if, perhaps, I'd imagined that scratch along his cheek. If, indeed, it might not have been all part of that conglomerate nightmare. But I knew it wasn't a dream and I also knew I was beginning that interior conversation about Nikki again: Nikki was ill, he was supposed to be well now, but I had to be patient and careful. He *must* be ill. This had been a horrendous mistake, coming back to the villa, and in my zeal not to seem overprotective, to help him feel self-reliant, I'd resisted taking the initiative. But I knew now I must. I had to get Nikki away from here before something very serious happened.

I looked out onto the gardens, almost a ritual since I'd arrived at the villa. The garden stretched away green and tranquil with that female cardinal who had obviously staked out this territory near the far corner of the terrace, darting in and out under the trees—a sliver of orange steaking though the green. From somewhere in the distance, came a rhythmic clicking sound as Sieppi went on with his business of trimming the hedges. What a peaceful pastoral this all appeared.

I tied a ribbon around my hair, which had begun to show the straggling ends of tossing and turning on my pillow, and sticking my feet into my clogs, went off to find Nikki. This had to be settled once and for all. We were going to return to the city immediately.

Boots had finished the vacuuming and was shoving the upright machine ahead of him down the long hall.

"Good morning, Boots," I said, feeling just a little self-conscious about the hour.

"Good morning, miss," he said, without turning, continuing to push the machine down the hall.

I knocked once at Nikki's door, waited, then turned the handle and pushed in. He was not there. His bed was neatly made and everything seemed in perfect order. Why . . . had I thought it would be otherwise?

I walked down the broad staircase and with each thud of my clogs hammering against the steps I kept telling myself: I won't be doing this much longer.

Outdoors the air was clear and refreshing with the scent of the villa's single joy, Sieppi's beautiful gardens. I could hear the sound of his clippers and followed it to him. He took off his hat and wiped at his forehead with a dark cotton handkerchief. I squinted against the bright sunlight.

"You look like Mama in the sunlight," he said. I could not pretend the sudden tearing in my eyes was the glaring sunlight. "Oh, Sieppi, thank you . . . thank you. What a lovely thing to say." He turned slowly then and peered out toward the hills below which, as we both knew, nestled that lake. Then he turned back just as slowly and looked at me with those limpid dark eyes in his sun-bronzed, aging face. He waited. I responded as though in some strange way Sieppi was drawing the words from me, willing me to respond.

"I'm looking for Nikki. I overslept," I added, in a feeble attempt to make some excuse as to why I seemed always to be looking for Nikki.

"I know. I see."

"I think, Sieppi, you see many things."

Maybe Sieppi knew now something more than he was saying, maybe he was trying to tell me something without saying it straight out. I chided myself for grabbing at straws.

"I see our boy is troubled. No good, sister," he shook his head. "No good. Take him home." He slapped his hat back on his head, picked up his shears, and attended his shrubs once again. I understood our interview was over.

"Thank you," I murmured and put my hand lightly on his shoulder. I felt sweat, damp, through his shirt.

I went halfway down the path toward the lake and stood watching the water gently lapping against the wooden boat dock, and the sunlight dappling lights and shades along the water's surface. I was acutely aware of the stillness, except for the cawing of a crow and the sudden flash of a wing fighting the air, catapulting from a tree. In the distance there was the sound of a lawn mower but otherwise nothing, as far as sight and sound could carry.

I found the stillness relaxing. The stillness in the house seemed ominous, an uncomfortable silence suggesting a prelude to some horror. I walked back up the path toward the gardens, toward the sound of the garden clippers and then, above that, the sound of an engine struggling to turn over. I turned slightly, trying to determine the direction of the noise. It was coming from the garage. Naturally, what more appropriate place for a motor to be turning over in than a garage? I walked in the direction of the garage and chauffeur quarters where I assumed Gretz would be working on one of the cars. The odor of motor oil and gasoline shimmering off the sun-baked macadam greeted me. Gretz, stripped to the waist, hunched over the Jaguar, oblivious to my footsteps.

"I'm sorry about the accident, Gretz. I hope Mr. Warton wasn't too upset."

"Oh, Miss Francesca, I didn't hear you . . ." He swung round, leaning his rump against the hood and wiping oil from his hands. "No real problem here. A little body damage and the timing is off a little but if you breathe hard on these temperamental babies the timing goes off so . . . as a matter of fact, we didn't mention the accident to Mr. Warton. Felt it might only upset him further . . . him not being too well." He paused. "Care for a drink?" he asked, pointing in the direction of a white iron table under a fringed umbrella where a tall bottle of collins mix and glasses with melting ice sat waiting for Gretz's respite from work. "Non-alcoholic, that is."

"No, but thank you just the same. Tell me, Gretz, has Mr. Warton been sick very long? You probably know more about him than I . . . we haven't kept too close contact and . . ." I trailed off with a flippant wave of my hand.

"Well, not really. Mrs. Dudley engaged me. I didn't see Mr. Warton but it was explained to me he wasn't very well. I wasn't told exactly what it was but just that he's sort of an old guy, and"—Gretz spun his index finger at his temple—"you know, sort of . . ." then, as if embarrassed by his remark, he stiffened. "Anyway don't you worry about the car. I'll put it straight in no time."

"Thank you, Gretz, I appreciate it." I wanted to pursue it a little more . . . to see if it was Mrs. Dudley who had suggested Phelps was a little senile or if he'd assumed that for himself but he had turned his back to me and lost himself to the car.

Turning from the garage I caught a movement in one of the windows looking out from Gretz's quarters. Looking up I saw Boots, his face partially shielded by the curtain, staring down at me. He dropped the curtain quickly and seemed to fall back into the room out of my sight. The movement startled me but as I walked along the yew-lined drive to the villa gates, I thought it was nothing odd for Boots to be there. I was sure there were many times when he sneaked off to some corner to rest or like me to escape Mrs. Dudley.

I reached the main road that wound its way through the Park and felt relieved at just these few moments away from the confines of the villa. I picked up a fallen tree branch and as I walked began peeling the bark. It was an almost unconscious gesture, and I remembered how often Nikki and I would walk along these Park roads, peeling and shaping such slender branches into magic wands. I had stepped off the road onto a narrow path opposite the villa gates that I remembered led to a narrow stream where we would try, generally unsuccessfully, to catch giant bullfrogs. They generally ended up a green shadow darting back into the water in a stream of bubbles only to rise again in the form of bulging, marblelike eyes on the surface of the water. I hadn't minded then but the thought of touching their slimy skin gave me a chill.

I'd gone much farther than I'd thought and was now on a small rise above the stream. It was much smaller than I remembered, little more than a trickle winding cautiously on a leaf-choked path. I was suddenly aware of a sound behind me . . . the movement of someone or something over the damp leaves and brittle twigs. I stood still. Nothing. But I had heard something. I moved again along the rise, following the shadow of a stream and heard the noise again muffled slightly by the thick, damp earth. I turned abruptly and the noise stopped. An animal . . . no . . . it would be scared and bolt . . . perhaps a child playing tricks. I started walking again leaving the path to cut through the woods to the road and the noise followed, louder now . . . if it was a child he was a long way from home, for the villa stood alone at this end of the road. I slapped at the underbrush, idly, with the twig, listening intently . . . the noise had stopped again. If it was a child perhaps he'd grown tired of the game. I stood still for another moment and got only stillness back. "Hello . . . is anyone there?" No response. Whoever it was or had been did not intend to make himself known. I shrugged as though to show anyone watching I was unconcerned, then, finding the going off the path a little too rough, moved back down to the stream to pick it up again.

The noise again. Footsteps I was sure. I turned to it and there was a blast. I fell back almost down the incline to the stream. Then another blast echoed through the trees toward me and I froze. I was on one knee, groping for a tree limb to pull myself up, my muscles squirming like eels under my skin so I felt I could not will myself to move. There was a great thrashing in the woods above me and a pain like a great gray shadow of cold fear pressed on my chest. They were gunshots . . . I was sure they were gunshots. I struggled up the incline to the path and ran blindly, not even realizing as the branches beat at my legs and face that I left a path for the woods until I stumbled and fell on a contortion of roots, hitting the earth as though it had shot up to grab me.

Stillness. As if the shots had been a final demand for total silence. I pushed up cautiously on my hands and knees then fell back in a choking grip of revulsion. There, almost where my head had fallen, was the contorted body of a rabbit, its hind legs still jerking in a fruitless effort to elude death, its brown fur moist with its own blood, and tiny bubbles of pink froth oozing from its nose and mouth. I shut my eyes against it drawing my breath in deeply to combat the nausea and staggering up fell into Boots's arms. I jerked away then almost instantly grabbed hold of him.

"Oh, Boots, it's you. I'm so relieved." I stood staring up at him and realized in that moment I was not really holding on to him; he was holding on to me.

"You should be careful," he grinned, "you could get hurt." He squeezed my wrists tightly so I squirmed to get free.

"Please, you're hurting me."

He let go with one hand. "What's this," he asked, almost pulling me after him to the dead rabbit. I closed my eyes as he kicked at it with his shoe. "Kids, huh . . . try and get a few kicks . . . see, you could be hurt if they missed."

"Please, I have to go. . . ." The sound of a car horn drifting down from the road drowned out my words.

Boots loosened his grip and turned to the sound, muttering something. I worked my wrist from his loosened grip.

"What's your hurry . . . where you got to run off to?"

I tried to salvage some sense of dignity.

"I've got to get back to the house. I've . . . I don't feel well. . . ."

"You don't look too good. I was worried about you . . . seeing you wander off like that . . . you and your brother . . . you two always wandering off. It ain't natural."

He was right on top of me as he spoke so that I had to turn my face from the beer stench of his breath.

"I was worried about you. Seeing you wander off down here. Boots he didn't want nothing to happen to you."

The car honked again.

"That's very thoughtful of you, Boots." I backed away awkwardly. "I guess I shouldn't have wandered off like this . . . I . . . But he wasn't listening. He had begun to walk back up to the road.

"You don't belong around here," he said softly over his shoulder. "You're a city girl, why don't you go back to the city?" And he was gone, leaving me to struggle up the path to the road . . . arriving just in time to see him slide into the seat of a white Chevy beside a young girl in hair curlers. They sped by me in a white blur—a very familiar white blur.

CHAPTER SIXTEEN

The villa seemed a cool and almost welcome haven when I stepped in from the terrace through the patio doors. The house was as still as the outdoors and seemed to exude an air of expectancy, as though indeed the house had drawn itself together and was waiting . . .

Well, one thing—it would no longer wait for me—Nikki or me. We were going home. Right now. I was halfway up the stairs when typically I bumped my sore ankle and winced as the clog flew down the stairs. I stood still, expecting the noise to bring someone—Mrs. Dudley or her husband—out to see what it was. No one appeared. I slipped off my remaining clog and in bare feet hobbled down to rescue the other one. Holding them in my hand I struggled back up the stairs, moving silently along the corridor with the clogs tucked one under each arm.

Everything about this house had become a threat and not a very subtle one. Surely there was no other way I could interpret Boots's remarks. The almost sadistic way he had spoken to me, the way he held me there, grinning that inane grin—it chilled me to think of it, like the sudden unexpected shock of a cold wind. Surely it was the work of Mrs. Dudley. Boots didn't even know us . . . all he did know of us would be through her. So much energy had been exerted to drive us away . . . to keep us from Phelps . . . to protect him or them or us, I couldn't be sure. I could only be sure of one thing, and that was that staying here any longer would be a mistake.

I dropped my clogs outside my room and padded barefoot down to Nikki's door and tapped. No answer. I rapped again, this time loud and sharply. When there was no response I turned the knob, leaned against the door, and went in.

Nikki was lying stretched out, his hands hanging loosely at his sides, eyes opened wide, staring straight up at the ceiling. My heart gave a sick lurch. For a moment—"My God, he's dead," I thought, and dropped to his side. His chest rose and fell. Thank God. "Nikki . . . Nikki . . . are you all right?" softly so I wouldn't shock him.

It took him so long to respond, to even turn his head toward me, I became frightened. My question was answered. He was very obviously not all right.

He lay staring expressionlessly, his arms spread by his side, only the slow rhythm of his breathing telling me he was alive.

When he did turn his face toward me his eyes were staring blank as though he did not see at all, as though, in fact, he might be drugged.

I put my hand out, caressing his cheek gently, as though to waken him from a dream.

"Nikki . . . ?"

"Sssh . . . listen . . . listen . . . Fran, I think I have it."

"Have what, Nikki?"

He patted my hand, a gesture almost as though to silence me. Then he rubbed his hands across his eyes and pulled his body erect. Sitting, head cradled in hands, on the edge of his bed, he said, "I can't explain. Not yet . . . almost." He took his hands from his eyes and looked straight at me. "It's almost like being within one step to the key of the puzzle . . . it's there—" he beat his fist in his hand. "It's *there, somewhere,* just eluding me, but I know it's there. I'll find it."

"Nikki, I'm trying to understand," I said, taking both his hands in mine. "Look at me, Nikki, we've got to leave. I'm frightened. I appreciate your struggles, whatever they are, even though I don't understand them but we've got to come to this one decision now. I cannot face another moment here—I won't even try to speak for you. You're your own boss. But you talked me into coming. I've been unhappy and frightened and Nikki—" I got up abruptly and stood leaning my backside against the bureau, my arms folded across my chest. I went on trying to sound as controlled as I could.

"I want to leave and right now. No, not later. And please, please, no excuses. Nikki, you know I'd do anything for you but I've reached the limit on this. I'm going to pack now. I'll help you pack and then we'll go. We're leaving." The words seemed to trip from my mouth before I'd even thought about them. I don't know where I got the courage from. More I don't know how I managed to insist on leaving without saying one word about my fears for *him*. But he might never have heard.

"I'll help you pack," I said as breezily as I could, moving

to the closet and dragging out his suitcase. He was standing now, by the window, his back to me so I hoisted the bag onto the bed. He seemed to be staring intently out over the trees, the gardens, the hills, toward the lake. I felt helpless watching him like that, captured by something he couldn't understand . . . searching for something more terrifying than he realized.

I took a few things from the closet and folded them neatly in the bottom of the bag. There was a shaving-gear bag by his bed and I carried it into the bathroom, emptying his shaver and colognes into the mouth of the soft brown leather. I picked up a nail clipper and a fresh handkerchief from the bureau and dropped them in too. His wallet lay open on the floor by the bureau, where it must have fallen. I picked it up, a strip of plastic-covered credit cards and photos falling out like a dangling accordion. I folded them back in neatly, glancing at one of Nikki and me as very young children in the living room of our parents' apartment. There was another of Nikki by himself that must have been taken in Europe. The third one made me start. It was Nikki and Joe, and in the background was Nikki's cottage at Brookhaven. I leaned against the bureau for support. Nikki and Joe at Brookhaven . . . why hadn't they told me? Why had Joe let me go on about Nikki like that . . . why did he pretend he knew so little about Nikki's problems? Was he making a fool of me or like everything else around here was there some other . . . more threatening reason? All I could think of then was that it must have been Joe out there in the rain . . . but I couldn't know what it all meant.

"Find something interesting. . . ." Nikki said coldly. He had moved from the window to the door. It was shut now and Nikki was dropping the key into his shirt pocket.

"Don't want Mrs. Dudley barging in with her grim reaper act, huh?" I tried to smile. He didn't answer. Just watched me as I dropped the wallet on the bureau then zipped up the shaving kit and laid it in his suitcase. I went back to the bureau, my hands shaking as I gathered a few shirts into my arms. Nikki was at my side so quietly I didn't notice him until he took the shirts and dropped them back into the drawer.

"Don't you want me to help you?"

"Sit down," he said, and the sound of his voice slid like ice over my back.

"Sit." He pointed to the bed.

I backed off and perched on the edge of the bed. Nikki paced in a semicircle around me, then froze, leaning against the wall, staring at me for what seemed an eternity so that I shifted uncomfortably under his gaze.

"Nikki, please." My voice sounded like an odd instrument on the room's stillness.

He didn't speak. My hands turned cold and I folded them into my arms.

"What has Mrs. Dudley said to you that is so upsetting . . . ?"

"I told you Nikki . . . she said that we were. . . ."

"What did she say about me, Fran . . . ?" He pronounced each word distinctly, overriding what I tried to say . . . and then leaned back on the wall to watch me.

"Nikki," the word struggled out. "Nikki. . . ." But I

could hardly speak, my body seemed to cave in around me squeezing tears.

He stepped into my shadow and lifted my chin firmly in the cup of his hand.

"Fran, tell me." There was no gentleness now. He was someone else, someone I had never seen before . . . and I realized then that I was afraid. Afraid of my own brother, I cried, falling back on the bed away from him, my crying distant, as though coming from someone else, surely not me. . . . I felt his hands reach to touch me and I pulled away curling up at the head of the bed, my hands squeezed in tiny fists under my eyes. "Please, what are you doing, Nikki, please." But all I could hear was Mrs. Dudley's accusation, not my own voice.

"I'm sorry," he said. "I'm sorry. I didn't mean to upset you. It's just that things are very difficult and . . . I am sorry." I slid off the edge of the bed pressing my clothes down with the palms of my hand. He seemed to have changed again, back to someone more familiar but still I felt so very alone.

"You must be right. I . . . we should go . . . we should . . ."

"Nikki," I swallowed. "Nikki, it's all right." I wanted to reach out for him, but didn't feel I could.

I stood with my hand arrested on the doorknob. I did not move. He came toward me, putting his hands on either shoulder. He said, "Listen, I'll never ask another thing from you, Fran, please." His fingers dug into my flesh. "I am *so* close, so close to the meaning of everything. Give me just a little more time then we'll leave. I can't leave now when it is all just within my grasp. I give you my word, Fran, we'll leave the first thing in the morning."

I could not answer. I did not know whether he was actually involved in something that would relieve his mind or whether he was simply retrogressing. Perhaps recreating, reliving, the whole awful experience. I wished desperately for someone—some other responsible person—to be with me. Help me.

CHAPTER SEVENTEEN

As no further mention was made about leaving and as I had not insisted we return, it was only logical Nikki should assume I had acquiesced. I would stay until the morning. I could hardly do anything else. I could not pressure Nikki because I felt I did not know whether pressure might be the one thing that would push him over the thin edge of stability. I felt sick with apprehension. When I'd closed the door to his room the image of Nikki slumped on the bed recalled the visit he'd made here years ago when they'd had to take him back to Brookhaven. Every line of his body had spoken of despair and dejection and he had been led away like a docile animal. This was the picture I'd taken with me now. I could not bear to see him like this. My poor Nikki.

So, I had agreed to stay and I felt now if Nikki had something to resolve I did too. I was determined to pick up on that meeting with Phelps and if, as it seemed, he and Nikki were both tortured by a buried truth, I would have it out with Phelps.

The corridor was empty, which meant nothing, for the Dudleys always seemed to appear out of thin air as though they were part of the house's very disturbing aura. I was surprised to find Phelps's door unlocked and, knocking first, pushed in. The curtains were drawn tight, so for the exception of a sliver of sunlight laying across the room, one would have thought it was night. I could barely distinguish a figure on the bed and moved cautiously to its foot, peering down its dark length. It was empty. The covers and pillow were bunched together in a careless mound and, putting my hand to the sheets, I could feel they were still warm. Someone cleared his throat. The inside of my body jumped as though it would lift me from the ground. I turned. Moving out of the shadows in the far corner of the room was Phelps in his wheel chair. He stopped at the thread of light, so it fell across his feet, leaving his face and shoulders in darkness.

"Oh." I let out a tiny flutter of air. "You startled me . . . I didn't see you when I came in."

"I'm sorry." His voice was soft. "I didn't mean to startle you. I'm glad you came. Mrs. Dudley told me you were leaving and I was afraid I wouldn't see you again. I haven't been a very good host, I'm afraid. I'm so sorry. So very, very sorry." He sounded almost childlike.

"I wanted to speak with you, too. I understand you're not feeling well . . . it's hard to be the ebullient host when you're feeling ill." I tried to be glib, thinking all the while how Mrs. Dudley maneuvered. She probably told Phelps we were running off without the slightest concern for him. "I wanted to finish our conversation . . . if you feel up to it."

"Perhaps it is best that you go." He didn't seem to hear me. "I was foolish, I think, to hope, to wish that things could be changed . . . that we could bring back the past and mold it so it wouldn't haunt us any more . . . foolish."

"Sometimes talking about it purges us . . . we clear the air . . . rid ourselves of the past," I prodded.

"Nikki may be better off than all of us. Not remembering. I wish I didn't. You couldn't understand that could you—that it would be better not to remember. It would seem part of your life has been robbed. After all, life is only memories, every act the moment we commit it, is a memory. There is no present . . . only the past and if that past tortures you. . . ." He drifted off, losing focus.

"What is Nikki better off not remembering?" I asked, trying to steer him back on course. I had a vague feeling of nausea toying with my stomach not wanting to really hear him . . . not wanting to hear again that Nikki had killed Mother.

"No . . . no. It is better I think that you go. I'm afraid he is not strong enough yet and that I will never be strong enough. Please ask him to forget. Please, it is so much better . . . please for him, for you, for me. For now . . . only for now. I am old . . . please." He tortured himself.

"Did Nikki kill Mother?" I blurted it out, wrenching it from my mind before I could control it, my body shaking.

"Oh, God," Phelps moaned. "Why can't you all forget . . . what good is this. Why have you brought it to this . . . what good have you done him . . . why . . . why. . . ." He screamed it, and I felt through my whole body that it was true.

The door flung open. Mrs. Dudley stood framed in the hall light. Phelps moaned, the sound running along my nerves until it clutched me by my throat and shook. I barely saw Mrs. Dudley race to Phelps. I barely heard her scream after me as I raced down the hall, slamming my door to her, to everything, falling on the bed and into hysteria.

I don't know how long I lay like that . . . a tight knot shutting out all feeling and sound until Aunt Virginia came to the door and knocked, speaking very softly. The first time I ignored her and waited for her to go away. The second time I answered. I heard her try the door. I had locked it.

"Francesca, are you all right?"

"Yes, thank you, Virginia, just tired."

"Oh, well, I won't disturb you, dear." I could visualize her, patting her coiffure daintily in place. "I—we—just wondered about dinner? Phelps seems quite indisposed and won't be dining with us—what about you and Nikki, dear?"

Nikki? I did not know where he was. "You and Uncle Willie go ahead, Virginia. I don't feel up to dinner and Nikki won't be back in time."

"Oh, well, in that case dear, Uncle Willie and I thought we might go down to Duck Cedar for dinner. It would make less work for Mrs. Dudley and it might be a bit of a change."

She tried the door again very gently. "Well, I meant if you don't mind our going. . . ."

"Of course not." Oh, why didn't they just *go* and *leave me?*

The next thing I remember it was morning! Morning of that day Nikki promised we would be going home.

Nikki! I sat upright in bed, the whole frightening scene with him and Phelps coming back to me. Nikki? He might even at this moment be on the verge of another collapse. He had been as confused and as irrational as Phelps. Why had I ever allowed him to come? I let him coerce me into coming and my misguided love and devotion to him would destroy him. I had to be the strong one. Nikki couldn't see things clearly when it came to the villa and our mother's death. He wasn't responsible. I ought to have been stronger. Oh, Nikki . . .

I fell off the bed. I knew what I had to do. I kept on the old jeans and shirt in which I'd slept. I could pack them later, but for now it was the quickest thing.

I went to Nikki's room first. He was gone and my heart sank. He had promised me. Promised we would leave. I couldn't face Dudley or Phelps . . . not alone . . . not again. If I could get Joe . . . if he would help. Surely he was Nikki's friend. Surely he would take him away with me. I walked swiftly along the corridor down the stairs and to the kitchen. It was empty and I hoped it would stay that way long enough for me to use the extension and get back upstairs to pack undetected. I lifted it from the cradle and heard Dudley's voice. I was just about to hang up when I recognized the other voice. It was Joe's. I cupped my hand over the mouthpiece and listened. Perhaps he'd called for me and I hadn't heard the ring from our wing of the house.

"Well, have you seen him this morning . . . ?" he was asking.

"On the patio . . . he seemed quite agitated. I told you sir, I didn't think any of this too wise, I fear. . . ."

"You've expressed your fears quite adequately, Mr. Dudley." Joe cut him off, sounding more blunt than I'd ever heard him. Apparently I was eavesdropping on a conversation about Nikki that I had nothing to do with. And apparently Dudley and Joe had spoken before. I was the outsider.

"Mrs. Dudley assures me they are leaving today. I hope it's not too late. I trust nothing tragic will evolve." I didn't understand what was going on. Joe and Dudley conspiring. I was a total fool.

"When are they leaving?"

"I don't know exactly, sir, shall I call you when I. . . ."

"No." Joe cut him off sharply and there was a click and dial tone. He had hung up. I could hear Dudley hang up too. I stood there, receiver in hand, hearing and rehearing Dudley and Joe. What could they mean to each other? I was going to cry. I could feel it at the back of my throat and in my eyes. Footsteps tapped along the corridor from the servants' wing.

I dropped the phone back in its cradle and turned just in time to see Mrs. Dudley, meticulous as always in her dark, uniformlike morning dress. I was startled to realize she had small cameo earrings dangling in her ears! Mrs. Dudley wearing jewelry. She must be planning to go somewhere in anticipation of our departure. She had stepped out of her starched domestic role and had begun to relax, I supposed. She was carrying a large floral centerpiece, destined for the dining-room table. She stopped when she saw me, edged the flowers onto a small side table, and came straight up to me.

"I trust you took my words to heart and that you've packed and are ready to leave." She drew a timetable from her pocket and thrust it toward my face. "You'll have no trouble picking out a bus. They leave on the hour every hour from Suffern. Gretz will drive you down. I've so directed him."

She'd directed him.

"How is my stepfather?" I asked, ignoring her and stuffing the timetable into my jeans. It was a question of desperation—something to say so I would not break down in front of her.

"He'll be fine once you two have gone. You'd better get going and be quick about it."

She leaned closer as she spoke her fierce little eyes glowed at me like some sickening reptile's. I felt repelled. I stepped back.

"When my brother returns I will tell him—tell him about your invitation to leave—and if he decides we should leave, then of course we shall." I was trembling inwardly as I spoke and I could feel the flash of sweat rising on the palms of my hands. "Until then—"

"You just better decide to leave," she interrupted, "or I'll tell everyone here—everyone you understand—just what your brother is—you'll see."

"What"—Nikki had come up close behind me and had his arm around my shoulder protectively—"what, Mrs. Dudley, will you tell everyone about Nikki, eh?"

I looked up at him. He looked as though he had been running, as though he had just come in from outdoors. He rubbed his hand along his forehead brushing an untidy lock of hair from his eyes.

Mrs. Dudley, without uttering a word, turned her back on us and marched off, the door of the servants' wing swung back and forth furiously long after she had disappeared, the only evidence she gave of her enormous rage.

"What was she going to tell everyone, Franca?"

"Nothing really . . . what could she tell? She doesn't know us—except when we were children."

I moved his hand from my shoulder, linked arms with him, and we locked hands and mutely moved toward the patio.

"Come on, Fran, you didn't look that panicked over nothing. What was it?" He held my chin, holding my face lifted toward his and stared into my eyes. I tried to look away. He held my chin firm.

"O.K." I put my hand over his. "It's just that she said we were fortune hunters we'd come here to wait for Phelps to die—she was so ugly about us. It—it frightened me," I lied. "Please—come on, Nikki, you promised. Let's go home."

I was trying to tug him in the direction of the house.

"No. No, Franca, that wasn't it, I know. I know what she means . . . it wasn't that—I think I know. I know I know. It's the answer. It's out there." Nikki pulled away from me and stared out over the trees, the gardens, the hills toward the lake.

"Come on, Nikki, you promised." I was cajoling now, pretending to treat everything lightly. "Look, I'll make a deal. Let's take off now. Then when Phelps is better and

Virginia and Willie have gone home we'll come back and square everything away. O.K.?"

He stood silent, looking toward the lake.

"Nikki, look, at least give it thought. Don't decide impetuously. Think it over, and in the meantime, in case you decide to take up my proposition. . . ."

"Go pack, huh? O.K. I will."

He took my hand and we moved up to the house. "It won't take me long to get my things together," he said, but Nikki's voice was somewhere else, as though it were moving out over the lake.

But I felt easier now, even moving up the stairs, knowing he would go.

"Do you want me to help you pack?" I asked.

"No. No, I'll manage. Just a few things. I'll stop by your room to take your things down," and he closed his bedroom door leaving me alone in the hallway and feeling suddenly very cold.

CHAPTER EIGHTEEN

I sat on the edge of my bed, a sudden wave of fatigue enveloping my body, as though the nervous energy that had carried me this far was suddenly deserting me. There was something in Nikki's manner, his contrived calm, his uncharacteristic willingness to leave, that made me uneasy. Suspicion, it was all foolish suspicion, I told myself, and I was making other people victims of my awful suspiciousness. But I had no one to help me. Nikki was too emotionally fragile. Phelps was sick and a confused old man and Joe . . . that hurt me so. Joe was what?

Sitting there I realized how tired I was, how little I'd slept or relaxed this entire weekend. But I couldn't afford that luxury until we were safely away from here. Yet, I felt I couldn't face that ride back alone with Nikki, I wouldn't be able to sustain a normal conversation all the way back to town without some help—now, especially with what I had locked inside me. But leaving would only be the beginning. Where did I go from there . . . ? Did I say to Nikki, Look this is what really happened. Did I go to his doctors . . . and let them decide . . . or did I just forget it and risk letting Nikki continue to struggle to recall that fatal day? That shock would surely be too much for him. I couldn't bear the thought of his facing that. I was frightened, too, of what it might do to him.

I lay back on the bed fighting the urge to cry. How could the delicate balance of one's life become so destroyed? I fought back my tears. I couldn't afford to lose control now, nor did I want Nikki to know I'd been crying. I sat up and searched in my pocket for a Kleenex, dabbing under my eyes and promised myself a good cry when we finally got home.

Nikki should be ready by now, so I tucked my shirt into my jeans and went out and down to his door and knocked gently. No answer. I knocked again, the sound reverberating down the long corridor. I pressed my ear against the door, straining for some sound that would tell me Nikki was all right. Nothing. I turned the knob, leaning heavily against the door so it swung open, catapulting me into the room. Nikki was gone. His bag, opened but empty, lay on the bed, his clothes still hung in the closet. He had made no effort to pack, and while I lay in my room feeling sorry for him, he had gone back out again.

"Oh, God," I groaned, leaning back against the closet door. I felt suddenly light-headed as though all the air was being sucked from the room and I had to struggle for breath. Nikki had said he felt so close to the truth . . . but I couldn't let him reach it . . . not now . . . not yet. I ran out and down the stairs steadying myself against the sweep of iron handrails. Mrs. Dudley loomed up at the foot of the stairs, arms folded, as though expecting me. "Did you see Nikki?" I asked, trying to keep the panic out of my voice. "He was packing and. . . ."

"Out," she said. "Both of you, out." She gripped my arm between her bony fingers and pushed toward the door. "You come here bringing your sickness and your sin. Take it and go!"

I could feel the words searing into me and I struck out wildly, unthinking, striking Mrs. Dudley flush on the face so she staggered back against the handrail, eyes wide, the sound of the smack reverberating, echoing back to me, grotesquely. She screamed at me, but I was already out the door and onto the lawn, the blood pounding against my eyes and ears. I hated her and I hated myself for losing control. I stumbled, sprawling face first, into a patch of earth freshly turned. Hands reached out, helping me to my feet. Dudley's hands, firmly guiding me and brushing a leaf from my hair.

"Why the hurry?" he asked gently.

"It's Nikki, I'm so afraid. I'm afraid he'll do something foolish if he remembers . . . if he finds out what really happened." And I pushed away. I hadn't meant to but some small frantic part of me twisted away from him toward the water. His voice trailed after me calling me back asking me to wait, but I didn't. I didn't stop until I reached the lake where it rose toward the boathouse.

"Nikki!" My scream was muffled by the ominous stretch of lush greenery reaching toward the water. "Nikki!" But only the gentle lapping of the lake against the land came back to me.

I started up our imaginary path, the narrow lane of bent weeds showing me where someone had just passed. The incline tightened my legs and seared my lungs, the dark, imaginary things of a wet, isolated woods grabbed at my feet, my tongue flecked at the edges of my dry lips, my throat ached with parched hoarseness. When I stopped, the blood beat more fiercely against my temples so that screaming out for him again shook through my entire body.

Above me the land leveled off, and from there, I knew, it would jut out, a contorted arm scarring the water's surface before plunging in a mass of rocks to the lake sixty feet below. That's where they'd found Nikki—or so they said—and that's where he'd believed he'd stood and watched his mother drown and that's where I was afraid he was now . . . conjuring up a buried memory from the quiet depths of the lake.

I saw his back bend to the sloping rocks and my voice hung in my throat as though it were already too late.

"Nikki," I called softly, afraid the sudden intrusion might startle him, "Nikki, are you all right?"

He turned, his face streaked with tears.

"Please, Nikki," I opened my arms. "It's all right." But my voice rang false like an adult consoling a child just old enough to realize it was not all right and probably never would be. "Nikki, please, come." I stretched my hand to him.

"I'm all right." His voice was hollow but strong, oddly strong. "I'm O.K."

"Move away from there, please. We can talk back at the house." I tried to keep the edge of panic from my voice.

"It's all right now. I know. I know now, you see. I knew if I was here I could get close, I've been close so many times. I felt I could put it all together." He was not looking at me but beyond or above me, to patches of blue gray in the rectangular pattern of branches arching over us.

"It's sad," he said, and my heart sank with the pitch of his voice. "It's sad when you come to the end of it. You act it all out again until you're sure you have it right and when you do you've freed a part of yourself but lost a part, too."

His voice was so controlled it frightened me, "Nikki, you don't blame yourself, do you? Please don't. . . ." I wasn't sure that was the right thing to say but I knew I must say something, though the wrong thing might shatter his strange aura of calm.

"Blame myself . . . ?" For the first time our eyes met. "There was really nothing I could do then. If I had remembered, things might have been different—at least clearer, though they're really not that clear now—now that I *do* remember." He studied his hands turning them over and over slowly as though seeing them for the first time. "It might have been better for us all if I'd never remembered. It's been so selfish, this driving desire to clear it up just for myself, but what have we really gained?"

"I don't really know, Nikki. It's for the best, I'm sure," I said weakly. I was confused by his reaction, if he really did know what had happened. "Nikki, come with me."

"Don't you want to know what happened?" He did not even look at me.

"Yes, of course, but not here."

"Why not here. Here. . . ." he waved, encompassing the lake and cliffs with the sweep of his hand, "the stage is set." A hint of hysteria had broken through his calm. "We lack only the players. We need . . . we need," he hesitated.

"Who else do you need?"

The voice came from above me. Dudley's voice, startling me at first, then reassuring.

"Dudley," I cried. "Please help." My voice betrayed my desperation.

He didn't look at me. "Well, who else do you need to complete the setting, Nikki?" he asked harshly.

"Our stepfather." Nikki's voice was weak, almost inaudible. "We need Phelps."

"Phelps?" My voice rose, quivering between them.

"Go on," Dudley said. "Why do we need Mr. Warton?"

Nikki studied him, backing off with his eyes. "You know don't you, Dudley? How long have you known?"

"I've always known."

"Why did you let me go on like this?"

"Will someone please tell me," I screamed.

"It's quite simple," Dudley said very calm, that deceptively sad, egg-shaped face looming above us. "Mr. Warton killed your mother. He took the other boat and tried to bring her back, she wouldn't come, they fought . . . they were always fighting. She went overboard and then he held her there. He killed her. It was that simple. Isn't that what you remember, Nikki?"

I didn't look at either of them. I was crying, not only at what I'd heard but, worse, what I'd believed about Nikki.

"Yes, that's it." Nikki's voice was very gentle. "You knew and you let me go through hell . . . why?" There was both anger and bewilderment in Nikki's voice.

"I had no choice."

WEEKEND AT THE VILLA

"No choice!" Nikki moved toward him. I clung to his arm.

"Nikki, I don't understand," I said.

"Stay there," Dudley's tone scared me.

"I want to know *why*," Nikki pushed my arm away. "You could have cleared up the whole thing."

But Dudley didn't answer. Instead he drew a pistol from his jacket pocket and held it waist-high and level, rotating it to encompass us both.

"Oh, Nikki!" I fell forward, burying my head in his chest. The whole thing was kaleidoscoping together uncontrollably, and to me, incomprehensibly.

He stroked my back firmly. "Dudley will tell us, won't you, Dudley?"

"I didn't want it like this but you forced it, coming here."

"We didn't want to come," I sobbed.

"That really doesn't matter any more, does it? It's been too long. And our demands were so small. But it's too late to turn it all back."

"Please, I don't know what you mean, Dudley. Nikki, what does he mean?" I was groping for any substance as to what was going on, something to tell me I shouldn't be afraid.

"He means blackmail, I believe, don't you, Dudley?"

"Not in the beginning, Nikki. I want you to know that. It wasn't until later. Years later . . . that . . . that anything came of it. I found you up here, Nikki, with your camera set up and I saw Mr. Warton on the lake, but then it was too late to stop anything. I realized later what had happened and when I developed your film I had almost all of it or at least enough to hang Warton, Mr. Warton. But I hesitated. They said you were in shock . . . and I hesitated. I should have spoken up, but I waited. I didn't plan then, at least not consciously, to use that film. I don't really know what we were thinking of. In a way I'd hoped you'd remember. It would have taken me off the hook. But you didn't. And it seemed you never would and the years went by . . . and finally . . . finally . . . we did go to him. We didn't ask for much. We don't work too hard when there are no guests. We have a little money and when he dies . . . well, we'll be taken care of. We're not greedy people, not really evil." Dudley sounded as though he wanted to believe that.

"Then why this now, Dudley, why the gun?" Nikki asked. He seemed to gain his composure as Dudley lost his.

"It's changed now. Coming here, remembering it all, has placed my wife and me in jeopardy. You see, Mr. Warton had a change of heart, that's why you were invited here. He had this compulsion to confess, to clean the slate, as he puts it, before he died . . . we couldn't have it that way. It wasn't the money any more, it was protecting ourselves. We wouldn't just be blackmailing then, we'd be accessories and if he opened the truth to you then we'd all . . . because of a senile old man's sudden. . . ." He struggled for composure. "Well, if *you* knew, the authorities would know, and you can see, we couldn't have that, now could we . . . I tried to reason with him . . . told him how it'd only turn you both against him, nothing would be gained and it was beginning to work . . . when you, *you* had to push and push." He raised the gun. "You would push it till you ruined it for us all. We tried to scare you off."

I thought suddenly, wildly, if I could keep him talking, if I could stall, time might work for us, help might come.

"How did you try to scare us off?" I demanded.

"In the chapel. That wasn't Nikki. I'd followed you as you followed him and I grabbed you to scare you off. You scratched my neck." He pulled down at his collar revealing a streak of red. "It was only coincidence he discovered you."

"Then those scratches on your cheek, Nikki . . ."

"You thought it was me! I got those running through the woods when you screamed."

"Oh, Nikki, forgive me," I closed my eyes against the scene, "and it was you at my window, too, Dudley."

"Yes, I planned it all."

There was a kind of triumph in his voice, like a man drunk with the wonder of his own brilliance.

"It was easy to get Nikki's clothes and even get them back in his room, while he slept, where you found them. A little drug to make him sleep and the suspicions people always have about someone, who's . . . er . . . been away like Nikki. . . . And Boots. He was so proud of himself. Why for a few dollars more he actually would have . . . well, I don't like to think of that. It all worked perfectly and he never knew a thing about it, but then you had to go and spoil it."

"And all the while I thought the worst. Oh, Nikki . . ."

"I thought you'd both leave. That you'd manage to talk Nikki into leaving before Warton got to you. Or Nikki remembered. Once you'd gone we could handle Warton. But it didn't work. You wouldn't let it work. So now this is the only way."

"Shooting us? Is that your way? How will you explain that away?"

"Oh, easy. It'll be suicide. We all know how tortured you were. Your aunt and uncle were so worried. My wife and me, too. You came up here, realized the part you'd played in your mother's death. . . ."

"The part I'd played!" Nikki screamed.

"Why, yes. Your sister knows. She even followed you up here, confronted you with it . . . that's why you had to kill her, throw her over the cliff and we can only surmise the impact of what you'd done became too much for your poor unstable mind and you killed yourself."

"No, it won't be that easy." Nikki pushed me aside and moved toward Dudley.

"No. No, Nikki." But he was out of reach as I stumbled after him.

"You'll have to shoot me, Dudley. That will be a little harder to explain, won't it?" Nikki was at the foot of the incline, his head level with Dudley's waist.

"If I have to do that I will, Nikki. It's gone too far."

I saw the movement behind Dudley before he heard the noise. When he did it was too late. Joe hit him at the knees, the two of them tumbled from the incline, the sound of their fall blocked by my screams. The gun dropped and

Nikki lunged for it, holding it over the two struggling bodies. I wanted to move toward them to pull Joe away, do something to help, but I was like a marionette without strings, gawking at their movements, struck immobile.

Nikki held the gun above his head and fired. The shot cracked loudly through the trees, shattering the lake's stillness. The commotion at our feet stopped and Dudley pulled away, drawing back. Nikki lowered the gun on him. "Joe. Joe . . ." he said, "you O.K.?"

"O.K."

I reached to help him, squeezing his hand as he stood. Looking at Joe, I didn't see Dudley's movement until I turned at the sound of the gunshot. He was staggering arms wide, reaching for Nikki, frozen, in a nightmarish stare until he staggered backward and down, down over the edge of the cliff to the mirror of water below.

"Oh, God. Oh, Joe." I clutched at his shirt, drawing him close to shut out all the horror.

"It's over now. O.K.? Nikki, Nikki, you O.K.?" Joe reached out, taking him by the arm and drawing him into a private circle, so our heads all touched with an air of conspiracy. "It's all over. It's O.K."

"Nikki," I apologized through convulsed sobs, "I'm sorry for doubting you. I did for a moment. And you, Joe. You and Dudley. You seemed to be so far and—"

"I made a little mistake, too," Joe said. "I worked with Nikki to make it on his own. To protect all of us I asked Dudley to keep an eye on him . . . you see I didn't know. But I decided to stay a little closer than the city . . . like a room in Suffern just in case things got a little out of hand." He laughed gently.

"Not now. Don't talk now," Nikki said softly.

I reached up to kiss his cheek. Then Joe, his arms firmly around us, led us slowly away from the lake.

CHAPTER NINETEEN

We were on the thruway, the last toll before the bridge, when I began to feel finally I could talk about it. The rhythm of the car enclosed the three of us together in mutual fatigue. Trust had almost lulled me into a kind of passivity.

"What," I asked diffidently, "do you think will happen to Phelps, Joe?"

"I honestly don't know. But I do know one thing."

"Which is?" Nikki asked.

"That it's over and done with now. And you can't worry about anyone else."

"O.K., doc."

I considered this some kind of flippancy, until Joe answered.

"Not quite, yet. Only a third-year resident, remember. When I hang up the shingle I'll charge you, and you better believe it."

"You mean you—" I could feel myself blushing. Would I ever get over the feeling anything I thought about Nikki and his illness that wasn't positive or cheerful was a kind of betrayal? I felt guilty.

"Uh-uh," he laughed. "I wasn't a patient. But Nikki was assigned me as an out-patient after he'd had a relapse and went back to Brookhaven and we sort of got involved in talking about this problem."

"Joe was the one who went to bat for me. We never lost touch, and he and I decided the time was right to unravel the whole thing. He felt it best if no one knew what was going on except," Nikki glanced accusingly at Joe, "except Dudley. Even I didn't know that he was a private spy."

"A double agent in this case," I ribbed. "I hope your character judgment improves or you'll starve." We laughed.

"If you can talk about it now, Francesca, I think you ought to know about the pieces Mrs. Dudley filled in for us. Phelps panicked. You see, he'd banked on his marriage to your mother—at the time she married your father—to get him out of his financial crisis. And, brother, was it ever a crisis! Bookmakers, racketeers of all sorts were after him. He'd been surviving on the 'promissory note' of his marriage to the Bascome millions. On the day of the tragedy your mother, quite inadvertently, discovered when one of the strong-arm men were there making their collections, that Phelps was also being blackmailed because it seems one of the goons who'd been pushing to collect before Phelps's marriage had helped Phelps's cause along by mugging your father—"

When I dropped my head down and put out my hand to Nikki, Joe said, "Look, shall we leave it alone for now?"

"No, no, I want to know. Let's clear it all up once and for always."

"In fairness to poor, misguided Phelps, he didn't know anything about that. He really hadn't anything to do with it. He found it out when the guys running the show told him his next step was to marry the heiress and that they'd cleared the way for him. That wasn't hard to do—marry your mother—old man Bascome played right into that game without realizing it. Well, after that the rest is easy to piece together. Your mother accused Phelps of murdering your father. Phelps panicked. He saw, then, as I imagine the Dudleys did, his whole life and world going down the drain." Joe shook his head. "Money, the love of which. . . ."

We were maneuvering our way through the city traffic now. Stopped for a light, Joe went on. "Dudley, as you know, posed as Nikki in the rain and—well, aren't you going to ask how Uncle Willie got involved?"

"Let's save it for later," I said, as we turned down into the Eighties and I knew my quiet little apartment was there, waiting. "I'm getting woozy trying to take in everything."

Later was when we'd dumped all the gear at the apartment. Nikki fixed Joe a drink while I showered and changed. When I joined them Nikki was stretched out on my white linen slipcovered love seat in his dirty old corduroys, finishing his drink. "If you don't mind," he said, "I'm going to shower and shave now and then hit the sack. I've had a long, hard day, as the saying goes."

"If you'll stop at my place while I change you can fix us both a nice dry martini—I use Plymouth, too—and then I'll take us to dinner," Joe said.

And that was just what we did. Sitting in a dimly lit

corner of the restaurant on the luxurious banquette, Joe explained. "It was a kind of round-robin of blackmail. You see, the visit your Aunt Virginia had made to Boston those many years ago was because she was pregnant. She had a son—"

"*That's* what she meant by Nanny!" I interrupted. "Never mind . . . go on with the story."

"Well, the baby died shortly after birth, but the Dudleys threatened Willie and Virginia with exposure if they didn't go along with their drive-the-Fabriolli-Grazzi-kids-home game. When all you have is a name and social contrivances it could ruin you. Then, too, there was the suggestion that you two would work your way into all the inheritance and cut Willie and Virginia out."

"Tell me something," Joe leaned over the table fingering his empty wine glass "isn't it a statistical fact that marriage between persons in the same profession—or the same avocation, if you will—have a lesser chance for success than most?"

"Marriage . . . who said anything about marriage?"

"Well, let's just say I like to have a good idea of where my competition is . . . or who it may be. . . ."

"As a for instance?" I knew that was an inane response, but I could feel my pulses began to race again and I thought this has got to be it! And all I could do was just smile.

"A for instance? Peter Wright as a for instance." The waiter came and poured the rest of the Montrechat and we lifted our glasses.

"Peter," I said, "is just a very good friend."

Joe's smile was dazzling. "Well, then, let us drink to all our good friends—and to us and our future."

We clinked glasses. "I'll drink to that," I said and my voice was barely audible. But he heard me.

Mystery
    Quintano   c.2

Weekend at the villa.

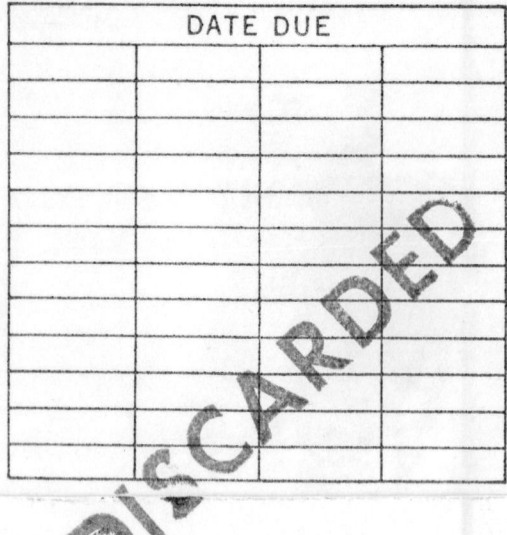

MANISTEE COUNTY LIBRARY
MANISTEE, MICHIGAN